MY KINDA GIRL

By
Michael McGrew

Published by Legacy Publishing Group

For information regarding special discounts or bulk purchases, please contact Legacy Publishing Group at legacypublishing11@gmail.com

Library of Congress Catalog Number: 2010914251

ISBN-13: 978-0-9830409-0-3

Printed in the United States of America

My Kinda Girl
Written by Michael McGrew
Cover Design: Davida Baldwin
Edited by: Arvita Glenn

ACKNOWLEDGMENTS

First, I'd like to thank time, because if it wasn't for it, I would have never discovered my true blessing. I'd also like to thank the streets of Los Angeles (the city that raised me), and when I say the streets, I mean the winos, dope fiends, OGs, single mothers, the squares, pimps, strippers, single fathers, whores, the losers and the winners, role models, ass kissers and kickers, corner preachers and teachers, and that's just to name a few.

It's the streets that raise us as youth, but we tend to lose focus and forget when we no longer need the same streets that taught us, to keep our heads high, and we can always fake it till we make it! A wino taught me how to tie my first tie on the street for my first job interview. I learned that a man's strength is only as dependable as his weakness from the dope fiends and their personal battles, but I never let their habit define them as people. The OGs taught me that regardless of what you represent, whether a gang or your reputation, you have to put your work in to get the respect you deserve from the crowd.

I was raised by a single mother and I never felt out of place or unwanted because of the absence of my pops. In fact, it proved to me that it's all about attitude and the way you perceive your lifestyle and expectations for yourself that determines if you would allow yourself to go down because of your lack of assistance from anyone. My uncle was a pimp and I learned from him that whatever attributes that you have in life to get ahead to maintain a status that compliments you, sets your individuality. There's nothing wrong with a man who seduces women and encourages them to do what they ultimately inquired within themselves in the first place; a pimp can never create a whore, he merely sponsors a prospect and brings the whore out of her; henceforth, proving to me that communication is everything you need to get ahead in life. I'm not condoning pimping, but just expressing the reality of the hood that I grew up in.

I'm also a single father and there are good men out there handling there business, and I learned from my experiences raising my son from birth, that sticking to something, whether difficult or impossible, defines the inevitability that greatness will prosper from it. My son is beautiful, and even though I sacrificed much and put my life on hold for him, instead of getting frustrated because I didn't have time for myself, I adapted to parenthood and lived through him, and I thank him most because he made me a better person.

Everybody plays a part in this world and nobody's better than the next, and you have to always respect each other's life that they either choose or were given. That being said, I am a product of my environment, but I chose what to withdraw, what I thought would be beneficial to me, in order to survive from my surroundings.

I'd like to thank God for giving me insight and the courage to take control of my creativity; my mother, my aunts, all of my crazy cousins, my pops, my son, the very few that I trust (you know who you are), and most importantly, the haters. If it weren't for them I'd probably think I was just average. Because it's when people talk about you that lets you know that you're doing something worth talking about, and that doesn't bother me at all; it's when they ain't talking about me that does!!

MICHAEL MCGREW
www.bookbizcoach.com
legacypublishing11@gmail.com

This volume is dedicated to my grandparents;
may they rest in peace.
We never know the history that surrounds
us until we are told by
someone else how much of an impact our
loved ones made,
and how important they were—to them!

Dear reader,
Grow old and appreciate every minute
of life with more smiles than frowns.

THE MIND OF THE MAN IS OFTEN UNKNOWN TO THE
MAN WHO HAS THE MIND

THE WILL OF MAN

After all the drama that I had been through, I thought this would be the longest and hardest day of my life. After six years in the Atlanta Federal penitentiary, I am due for release in the morning with one thing on my mind: a nights rest. I was awakened by my noisy and obnoxious neighbors, and started my day by washing my face and brushing my pearls, when I suddenly found myself staring at the stainless steel prison mirror.

Something was different about me; and six years of reflecting on the time I've wasted in here has caused for a new and improved version of Bobby Williams to emerge successfully into the real world. My young face reminded me that time was still on my side and at twenty-five years of age, opportunities were still in my favor. I promised to never return.

My motivation to do the right thing was the reason my heart continued to beat. I'm just glad that I was fortunate to make it, unlike others that I've seen parish between these walls during my stay here. Waking up everyday in a cell is a nightmare, but I'm finally done. I'm ready to resurface and claim what's mine; not the world, but just my own imprint.

Money, clothes and fast cars was all I ever wanted in life. And I did everything I could to get them. I was forced to grow up early and learned what corners to cut, opposed to which ones to walk around in these streets. The Dirty South is what we're nationally known as, and swag is everything. But everyone's not hospitable—if you dig what I'm saying. You can lose your life for a simple misunderstanding out here. And I've been in my share of situations that opened my eyes wide enough.

Everybody knew me as a hustler, or an opportunist looking for a come up however I could. Whether it was shooting dice before, during and after middle school, or breaking into homes in high school, I've always had a fascination with money and how it worked.

In my hood, like others, options were limited to more risky and illegitimate adventures to get rich; and getting an education just seemed in the way of accomplishing that goal. Ever since I was knee high to a fire hydrant I've been a good talker. And I hate to brag, but I could sell sleep to a dead man!

When I woke up this morning I could have swore I heard my mother's voice—May she rest in peace! However, it was the deputy telling me that it was my time to ride. The process of my release was approximately two and a half hours; but I didn't mind the wait. It gave me some time to reflect a scene in my life that often reminded me of a movie. If I were asked to label my life, with no hesitation, I would say hazardous. I was the youngest of three kids; one brother and a sister. My sister, Pamela, was my twin and was only three minutes older than I; and Brilliant was already three when we came into the world.

My mother used to tell me how she could have slept through Pamela and Brilliant's birth—but not mine—I gave her the most pain as I came out kicking and screaming. She was a very spiritual and loving woman with an unusual sense of humor, but with all the ass-whippings that I received as a child, I definitely didn't see anything funny until I was an adolescent and asked her about our names. She'd said that she named my sister after her favorite seventies soul, super-hero Pam Grier. My brother was named Brilliant because he was born in a church, and I was named after the proclaimed king of R&B, Bobby Brown. When I asked why, she said, "Because I knew that you were going to be a bad ass when you came into the world."

I attended my first of many funerals when I was eight years old, and losing friends became unnerving as I got older. When you're from the hood, funerals become casual get-togethers, and there's always one less person than the last. Walking up to view the body was always the hardest part. And most of the time I just did it because everybody else did. I guess you never know how serious a funeral is, or experience that unbearable pain of absence, until it's someone you actually love. And just when I thought I could get through life without experiencing a similar tragedy, my number was called to shed bigger tears just a few years later.

We weren't necessarily the Cosby's growing up, and mom tried her best to hold our household together, but things got a little difficult for her as Pamela got older. Even though her issues were overlooked by her beauty during her middle- to teenage years, our father's absence has always influenced her to look for a man's love outside of our household.

It all started with our father fading out of the picture during our eighth grade graduation; and even though it affected us all, it devastated her the most. Men doing what he did made life a lot harder on a family—period. And it severely dis-figured ours. Our mother struggled with two jobs while dealing with her beautiful baby girl, soul sister heading into the wrong lane; making un-healthy and careless decisions that they debated often.

"Pamela Williams, get over here right now! What is this?" I remember mom saying when she went through her bag and found a condom. She flipped out; and I would too if my fourteen-year-old daughter was having sex.

"What are you doing going through my stuff, mom? Damn! It's not mine," Pam said, and I could here them from the living room.

"Yeah, and I'm Peggy peg head! You are my daughter; okay? You come from my body and I know when you're lying and telling the truth."

They usually went back and forth like that all the time; and I knew Pam hated being monitored and just wanted to make her own decisions.

She moved out for the first time at fourteen, and in with our aunt. Mom didn't take too kindly to it at first, but she came to her senses after noticing how peaceful the house was now that she was gone. Pam had an overprotective attitude, and always stopped by with a little money to give. But mom never accepted *the devil's money,* as she clearly expressed her concern about where it came from.

As Pam got older, her reputation was far from an honest living and it strained the relationship between them. I remember hearing them argue one night, and this time was different than the others. That's when she found out that Pam had had an abortion; after eavesdropping on a conversation Pam was having with her man.

"I made it to my mom's house, baby. I feel so bad right now for going through with it, but having a baby would have made our situation extremely difficult for me. What was I supposed to do?" Mom heard her as she entered the kitchen and Pam quickly ended the conversation in tears. Mother was against taking a life in any way, and had a strong opinion about the subject of abortion.

"Did I just hear what I thought I heard? I raised you better than that! No daughter of mine is going to be proud of being a whore. You're a baby killer who needs Christ. Why are you doing this to yourself? Where did I go wrong with you, Pamela?"

Pamela genuinely loved our mother and never meant to intentionally hurt her. She just took it upon herself to do what she had to do to survive. I guess the guilt of her actions overwhelmed the game she learned to play in the streets, and she knew a change just had to come.

"You don't understand, Mom. Let me explain" Pamela responded out of shock after finding out that her conversation was not so private.

"No, Pamela, you've hurt me for the last time. I can't continue for you to influence Bobby any longer. You know he looks up to you, and I'm not going to lose two of my children to the system. As much as it pains me to see the direction that you're going, I don't want to see you again if the devil is still with you."

Pamela was speechless. With a look of resentment she had no choice but to pack her belongings for the last time, and find a way to survive completely on her own. I found out later when I came home what had happened, but I knew they were bound to finally bump heads. A couple of months later I left the bird's nest and moved in with my girlfriend. I was eighteen years old.

My brother really reminded me of our father and took after him the most. Sometimes I think mom favored him most because of it, too. When I left home I never looked back. And as a young adult I traded in the dice and small-time con games for a hunger to be rich and famous beyond my dreams.

At that time I didn't have a clue how; all I knew was that I wanted all the nice things that my favorite rappers talked about—even if I had to take it. I saw myself running a business one day; like a record label or something affiliated with the industry. That's where the money is.

Brilliant was leaving for boot camp and his ride canceled, so I took him. And besides, I loved being around him. He was already behind when I got there, but I managed to hit a couple back streets. But he looked bothered.

"What's up, man, you having a change of heart about being all you can be?" I said jokingly.

"Mom's got bone cancer, man. She didn't want me to tell you or Pam because she didn't want ya'll to worry. Don't bring this up, man, she'll kill me," he said. I definitely didn't expect to hear what I'd just heard, and really didn't know how to respond.

"Cancer? Get the fuck out of here; you're kidding me, right?"

I was hurt that she wanted to keep this from me and felt left out, as if she didn't love me enough to share something so personal with me. I became so overwhelmed with sadness and disappointment that I had to unbuckle my seat belt before continuing. "How can mom get cancer? She doesn't even smoke. I've got to go see her after dropping you off."

"I knew I should've let her tell you. Well, you needed to know anyway. Oh, and when you see Pam, tell her I love her," Brilliant said.

We pulled up to the terminal and I hopped out to help him with his bags. I was happy to see him doing something with himself, even though I wouldn't have made that choice. Before he walked away to check in, he asked me a question, "Hey, Bobby, I got a letter in the mail about a court date that I missed. Did you use my name or something?"

"I don't know what you're talking about," I responded. But he knew it was me. I reached in my pocket and gave him a hundred dollars.

"Have a safe flight, bro, and call me when you land all right."

"Cool and thanks—I'm just asking because I'm having some legal issues that I'm dealing with right now, so it wouldn't be a good idea. Kiss mom for me, later."

It wasn't until we explored our own horizons that I clearly understood how much mom struggled to raise us after our dad left, and she earned every ounce of my respect. And I guess the cancer decided to fill the void of our absence.

Without the responsibility of taking care of her children, she began to let herself go. She had no interest in going out anymore, so I stopped trying to persuade her. Maybe she was happy with her cooking shows and good reads. I would've known if I ever paid attention. But I promised to do so from now on. I didn't think anything else in life would measure up to watching her in pain the way she was, at least that's what I'd thought.

THE CON IN ME

Being a young adult, my mentality was something of an elder. It's like I understood human nature so well that I could practically read people's minds, and manipulate them to do whatever I required. What I learned so far was everybody wanted something for nothing, and without money—the liquid—our rivers won't flow. Money is everyone's motivation and without it, you're just dead water.

Following my intuition was my secret to the getting the money I had saved so far. It wasn't much, but I was stable enough to get the woman I wanted and the respect I needed. With good looks and common sense, you'd be surprised how far you can go. I learned these things in my earlier years watching the guys in my neighborhood. And if my mom knew I was running packages for a local dealer, she would have buried me in something hollow for real!

Little did I know that I was getting educated in another fashion, and I loved it. My sister used to tell me that the game was something that squares would never understand, and street smarts would get you further in life than a book would.

I was a natural salesman and selling dreams was my number one product. I also ran many con games. There's one in particular that I can never forget: I used to act like a tourist leaving the airport and looking for a cab. Once I found a target, preferably male, I would give him this story about moving from Florida to move in with a girl that I've been having a long-distance relationship with who I met online. That was always my story.

"Where are you going, sir?" the driver asked before activating the meter.

I passed him a paper with directions on it. "Can you take me to this address? I'm from Florida and don't know my way around, but that's where I'm going. Thanks, sir!"

To run a con, what you're doing is basically playing someone's greed against them. Once I gave him the directions to the location, I already knew that he was going to take me through the city before I got to my destination; but I needed that amount of time to plant my seed.

"So what brings you to Atlanta?" the driver asked; which is typical for a taxi driver.

"Well I've been talking to this girl for about six months now, and I'm moving out here to move in with her. She is so awesome and I think I love her."

"You don't think that's a big step? I mean, have you ever met her in person at least once?" he asked as if he was concerned, but in actuality, he probably thought I was the dumbest guy on earth. Exactly what I wanted him to think.

"No, and even though my friends and family think I'm moving too fast, she makes me feel so good about myself and I want to be with her.

11

How is it out here?" I asked shortly after pronouncing how gullible I truly was. He was hooked and I can tell how he could take advantage of this out-of-towner.

"It's a great city and developing a lot. You might get in trouble with all of these beautiful women out here. Okay, sir, this is your location on the right; it comes up to seven dollars and ninety cents."

By the time we got to the address that I predetermined, the driver believed I was young, dumb, and full of cum; an eager yet naïve, young stud who thought with his dick and not his brain. All I needed for this con was a dummy roll, an envelope, and cut up pieces of newspaper, intended to fit the description of a match: a stack of money. A dummy roll is a wad of money, mostly dollar bills with a fifty or one hundred-dollar bill on top.

"Hey, baby, I'm in the front and about to come up, are you coming down?" I asked on the phone.

I paused for a second as I listened, holding the phone slightly away from my ear so that he could hear the female's voice. "Okay, baby, well, I'm in the shower, so come up to 4B and my brother will get the door."

"Oh, okay, well tell him I'm coming up now." After ending the call I looked at the driver with a look of concern.

"What's wrong? Aren't you happy to finally be here?" he asked. What he didn't know, was that the call was setup, and now it was time to move on to phase two: the money transaction. In order for me to accomplish this, I had to make the driver believe that he was the only person I could depend on at that moment, which gave him leverage to take advantage of me.

"Well she never mentioned having a brother, and this is the first time I'm finding out about any siblings. I think she's trying to set me up or something. What do you think?"

I showed the cabbie my fat stack and gave him the long face about bringing my life's savings with me, which equaled thirty-five hundred dollars, along with the clothes on my back to make a living with the girl of my dreams.

"I have an idea. I just want to make sure I'm not left high and dry when I get up there. Can you help me out?" I asked and he was eager to hear my proposition.

When curiosity intrigued the cabbie to inquire about his benefit, he anxiously spoke the words that confirmed his interest.

"Right now you're the only person I can trust. And I'm not too comfortable walking into that building with thirty-five hundred dollars."

"You've got thirty-five hundred dollars on you now? I can understand why you're so skeptical. Well what do you need me to do?" he asked as he turned around to speak instead of looking through the rearview window.

"I want to know if you can hold this envelope while I go upstairs to assure my safety." I put the money into an envelope and sealed it for him to see, before I lowered it out of his sight.

"Sure no problem!" he said, expecting for me to just hand it to him like I was born yesterday.

"But, sir, you've got to at least meet me half-way because how do I know that you won't drive away as soon as I go in there? Okay, how about I pay you five hundred dollars to wait here and hold my money until I get back? But you have to give me some collateral like an ID card or some-thing, so I'll trust you more; or just give me whatever cash you have in your pocket and I'll give you twice as much when I get back."

He reached into his pocket and pulled out some cash quick. "Um, I don't have a card but I've got four hundred dollars. So you're telling me you're going to give me eight hundred dollars when you return if I hold your savings for ten minutes?"

"Exactly; just a token of appreciation for hav-ing my back. So what do you say?" I asked while handing him the envelope. Unfortunately, I had switched it with another envelope that contained only newspaper clippings, when I lowered the money previous to him agreeing to the terms of our deal.

It never failed, so I knew this greedy bastard planned to leave as soon as I walked into the building. They always drove off breaking the speed limit like they just pulled off a successful caper, only to find out when they got home, how stupid they really were. Being a good liar is very difficult and it takes a lot to deceive someone. But I felt bad after this one, because this driver actually waited for me instead of taking off as usual. After meeting up with a friend in the back of the building after walking in, we drove around the corner and noticed him still waiting for me to return. Sadly, I wasn't, but you can never hate the player, just the game.

In a single day, I usually banked one thousand to fifteen hundred dollars. A con like that required extensive travel, but whenever money is involved, does a few extra miles really matter? Since I had a pretty good turnout for the day, Brilliant, Pamela, and I decided to take our mom out for her forty-first birthday. Despite our differences, we managed to enjoy ourselves together. We shared our first drink together that night before we took her to a Tyler Perry screenplay at the Lakewood Amphitheatre in Atlanta.

Thinking back at that particular moment almost made me realize how much of an impact my mother was on me, and I noticed at that point, that as her child, she didn't want too much: a simple conversation about her favorite show, my day, a compliment, and time. The show reminded me of how we used to be. Brilliant cried during most of the singing segments and still denies it until this day.

Over the years I've learned that appreciating time is the best gift that you can offer. Unfortunately, my mother wasn't alive to experience my revelation and the memory of that day will always remain special to me. My sister dropped out of the picture for four months after the funeral. It was unlike her to do that. Then one day out of the blue I received a call from her, and even though I was excited to hear that she was okay, she sounded disturbed, and once again, I began to worry.

"Hey, twin, I'm sorry for disappearing off the face of the earth, but I've been running in circles trying to get my life together. It's a long story but it's nothing that your sister can't handle. Anyway, I have to speak with you, so what are you doing in an hour?"

"I'm not doing anything. Let's meet at the Sundial for some drinks and you can tell me all the drama you want, if you got me on the first drink." We both laughed.

It tickled my heart to hear her voice once again, and immediately after getting off the phone, I hopped in the shower before getting dressed. She was my other half and without her in my life, life itself just didn't make sense at all.

She arrived shortly after I walked in and I was over the top when I saw her. She looked gorgeous and after pulling out her chair, like a gentleman, she declined the menu and ordered two shots of Patron and an artichoke dip appetizer.

"So do you miss me or what?" she said, opening her arms before jumping up from the chair and hugging me.

"Of course; where have you been? You look good. How is everything with you?"

"I'm doing better than yesterday, but not as good as tomorrow, Bobby." She grabbed my shot of Patron and took two sips before the shot glass was empty. Her eyes were racing as if her heart and brain were having a private meeting, as she began with details about a man she'd met two years ago named James Fullerton.

She opened her hands revealing her palms, before speaking, "I have the best of both worlds in these palms, but I can no longer juggle two lives. James is a highly-motivated and charismatic man from Buckhead, who wants to take care of me.

"I mean his world is so unfamiliar to mine, but he influences me to believe there is another world out there for me. He's financially straight but he is more consumed with his business than he is with me, and Millertime is all about me. I'm in love with two men but I can only be with one, you know?"

"Millertime?" I asked, and Pam laughed before explaining.

"You'll remember him if you see him. I brought you over his house a couple of times and you used to play with his son."

"So what are you going to do about this sticky situation? This James guy sounds cool, and even though you might like Millertime, I still want to see my sister doing better for herself. The streets never loved anybody, and many of us don't get an opportunity to get out, maybe this is a life changing opportunity for you."

As soon as the waitress brought my appetizer Pamela received a call, and I could tell by her facial expression that our reunion was coming to an end sooner than I expected.

"Why, what's wrong, babe? Okay, I'll be there in a few . . . Okay, I'm leaving now." Pamela seemed frustrated when she ended the call.

"Hey, I just have to end the drama and I swear we are going back to how we used to be. Thanks for the advice, and I know my decision will set me free. I'll call you later tonight." She went into her purse and grabbed twenty dollars and put it on the table, before kissing me on the cheek and leaving.

"I love you, sis. Don't forget to call me. I've got tickets to the hair show this weekend."

I stayed behind for a little longer and ordered the beef tenderloin and wild mushrooms, as I looked over the impressive skyline and wondered about the years to come. It had already been four years since my graduation, and I couldn't say the world was coming to an end, but life for damn sure had to get better soon.

The next morning as I lay in my bed, tempted to initiate a quickie from my arm charm, I received a call from a number that I did not recognize. A masculine voice stated, "This is Detective Frank Chaplin with the Decatur City Police Department, may I ask who this is?"

"This is Bobby Williams," I replied curiously.

He then continued, "Okay, Mr. Williams, I'm calling in regards to a homicide victim, a Ms. Pamela Williams, and considering that your last names matches, it's only natural for me to assume a relation, correct?"

It took a while for me to answer as the news of my sister's death registered to my brain. "Yes, I'm her brother. Who did this and how did you get my number?"

"Her cell phone was located when her body was discovered, sir. And we're searching for any possible suspects. If it's possible, sir, I'm going to need you to identify the body. Do you need to know the location of the deceased?"

"Yes, please."

"Okay, it's 3620 Piedmont Road. Thank you, and sorry for your loss," he said.

"I just saw her last night. This can't be happening. I'll be down there as fast as I can. Have you found anybody or anything yet?" I asked almost in tears; and even though I hated law enforcement, at this point, he was my best friend, since it involved catching my sister's killer.

"Well so far, after your number, a few restricted calls were made and we don't have any leads this minute. But we're working diligently to put whoever did this in jail for as long as they live." The officer seemed determined, just as I was, but I wished that I wound find this person before the law did.

I rushed out of the house and went straight to the address he'd given me, to identify Pam's body. I was on edge and couldn't think straight at all. When I got there it was chaotic, and up until the detective lifted the sheet for me to identify my twin sister, I prayed that it wasn't her. But unfortunately, it was, and half of my spirit instantly became soulless. The detective had mentioned that there was no forced entry, and considering her previous history as a known prostitute, which was new to me, it was leaning towards being ruled a crime of passion.

That did not sit right with me.

I'd spoken to Pam often outside of that four-month window, and told the detectives about her new life and change of heart. "She had new goals and plans for herself," I proclaimed.

After they transferred her body to the hospital, the coroner said she died fighting—as if that would have eased my pain.

After realizing the depth of my loss, I began to shed enough tears to carry Noah's ark. Detectives are so rude with their questions and insensitive approaches. It was routine to them and they even tried to act sincere with their promises to bring the killer to justice. However, due to the high-crime volume, the case was easily overlooked.

The funeral was in preparation. Until this day, I really missed my sister, and now two of the most important women in my life were gone. Mom always said, "Everybody's life was like a railroad track and could shift at any point. God gave us the gift of option. It's just up to us to choose. Some hold us back and some push us forward." Obviously, her course was planned by an undetermined factor: obsession.

At the funeral my sister looked bothered, as she lay in her ash solid-wood casket. A life interrupted for reasons that couldn't be explained justifiably with a clean conscience. I needed an outlet; and if I knew the killer's family personally, I would advise his mother to invest in a black dress of her own.

I saw a lot of people at the funeral that I had no idea my sister socialized with. A couple flings, to say the least, and her new boyfriend, James Fullerton. He approached me with the confidence that I would be interested in what he had to say. If I only would've known then what I know now, my reaction would've been, let's just say . . . a little less easy going!

After introducing himself, I started asking questions, "Pam told me about you the day she was killed. That's kind of ironic, don't you think?"

James took his hands out of his pockets and placed them together before speaking, "I loved Pamela more than I loved myself, but she had skeletons in her closet that I couldn't compete with. I tried to separate her from her past in order for her to move forward with a more rewarding lifestyle with me, but her secrets . . ."—James squeezed the bridge of his nose with his thumb and index finger in sorrow before continuing—"her secrets, whatever they were, ate her up inside, and now she'll never live to best of her potential. What did she do to deserve this? I miss her a lot."

Things were becoming a little clearer to me as I tried to put the pieces of Pam's secret life together, and my assumption so far, was that whoever killed her definitely had a motive.

BE CAREFUL WHAT YOU PRAY FOR

"I know who killed her, Bobby," he said under his breath; and I wasn't expecting to hear that at all. It sent chills down my spine because I'm not used to my wishes coming true—whatsoever, and finding my sister's killer instantly became a priority on my list.

"What do you mean you know who killed her?" I demanded. I was loud enough to alarm an older lady next to me, and knew it was time to leave if we were going to discuss this any further. I didn't know this guy too well, and it pissed me off knowing that he was more informed than I, her twin brother. I wanted revenge and I wanted it now! After relocating to a more secluded area we continued, "Okay, tell me everything. And please don't disappoint me."

"His name is Millertime. The champagne of pimps whose sole purpose in life was going hard on the women who worked to make his pockets grow—a real pain-in-the-ass criminal with no regard for human life. I tried to remove your sister from that life and she told me to let her take care of him, and when she tried to end it with him, this is what happened. I can't go to the police because . . . well, I just can't go to the police about this, but I know that he hangs on the eastside," James said in absolute caution of his words.

"So what you're saying is my sister was a hooker who was murdered by her ex-pimp? You know, this isn't the best time to offend me, man."

Then he went on to tell me things that I never knew, but had to be true, about this guy. The more I thought about, it all made sense to me, and her absence backed up his story so far, and I'm sure mom was aware of her troubled life back then.

The more I heard, the more I wanted to put him to rest. I knew his type and had friends just like him. Millertime was a low-down, rat-soup-eating waste of human flesh that cruised the streets of Atlanta in his honey-mustard yellow Range Rover, on twenty-two inch Asanti rims. Making frequent stops checking corners, talking shit, and swallowing spit with his player partners.

Millertime and my sister had a history that ran deep. They were almost identical with their inability to settle for an average life in the ghetto. "It's all about making your next step your next step," he used to tell her as he influenced her to use her sex appeal to close a deal.

He then went on to elaborate about his beliefs, leading her to believe that sex is another form of communication with breathtaking analogies like: "Love ain't nothing but two people feeling sorry for each other."

Reconfiguring Pamela's perception was considered an investment to manipulate her feelings and make her believe that he was the only man for her. At twenty-two, she had the total package. My sister had a good head on her shoulders, and was smarter than most of the men she dealt with. Pamela had a body that other women would die for, and made men fall at her feet. Her measurements were thirty-six; twenty-four; thirty-six. What the old-timers used to call a brick house. Her eyes were golden brown, and she had the complexion to match.

Pamela had the kind of full lips that led men astray with their lame attempts to present anything other than money. Her curly short hair illuminated her presence, and was topped off with the sexiest birth mark on the side of her face the size of a bottle cap. It didn't take too long for Millertime to see that she would increase his pimp status tenfold. She defined fantasy!

Even though Millertime concealed his feelings toward Pam, there was only one focal point that would reduce her to an expendable asset, his frog skins. Pam quit her job the next day and when asked why, she said that she found a better boss! Listening to James's version of Pamela's interaction with street niggas answered the question that I wanted to ask her at that time, but overlooked due to my own preoccupation in the streets.

It was a long night; and a long night turned into my own sharp pain of absence. I focused my eyes before I looked at my Movado to see what time it was. In a four-minute timeframe, I had a four-year flashback and desperately needed a drink.

"I'm going to need you to let me know everything you know that Pam was going through; and since you were the only one close to her in the last four months, your history with her can help me find Millertime." This was the hardest thing for me to deal with so far and I broke down in front of James.

I buried my face in my palms as they played a sponge to my tears. I remembered Pam mentioning this Millertime guy, and I hoped he didn't think someone wasn't looking for him already.

"So tell me more about this Millertime guy?" I asked with all the aggression that my body could muster.

"Millertime wanted your sister so bad, and just couldn't accept the fact that he was her past and I was her future. I told her to get a restraining order but she didn't listen, and I knew for some reason that he would do something harmful to her. That bastard should pay for what he did, and I'm sure you think he should too."

James was very edgy and kept repeating himself, and it bothered the hell out of me. I just wanted the facts so I could rid the earth of his chicken-hearted, greasy, ill-mannered presence.

We excused ourselves after the funeral and went straight to the bar. James seemed like a very organized guy. I knew then why my sister would have fallen in love with him. He said they were in love and planned to get married. After a couple of shots and some wings, the rage compelled me to search for Millertime immediately, but I had to play it smart. And like I've heard before, *I've got to keep my enemies close,* and James surely wasn't off the hook yet. We talked and talked until we damn near knew each other completely, and I have to say that I was impressed with his business savvy.

"I started a record label and I'm trying to get it off the ground, and I could use some help. I'm working on a plan to get the capital to run it so I have that covered. All I need from you is to help me organize and run it. What do you say?"

"Man, that's what I'm talking about! I've been making some calls and know some rappers who are making noise. Let's get it."

We took a couple more shots down before leaving, and exchanged numbers in case I needed more info on Millertime. Besides, wc had a record label to invest in. We were drawn to each other immediately as if we were meant to be friends. We were associates with a bond, which was the love for my sister and a secret, which was a murder was about to go down.

The detective called me a few days later and told me that James's story had checked out, and his alibis matched; so I had no reason to believe that he was a suspect. A week after Pamela's death, I had all the information I needed to know about Millertime. Since he was a known pimp and his business was in women, I decided to make a move and hired a prostitute who was new to the streets and hated pimps with a passion. After a brief conversation, she persuaded Millertime to follow her.

"Hey, superstar," she said with an inviting tone. It caught him by surprise because he was usually the first to initiate.

"Do I know you, baby? I like your style and I can tell we're playing the same sport, but we're in different arenas."

"And what arena is that, sweety?"

"The arena of pimpin', so vote or die, baby. Who are you working for?" he asked as he walked close enough to smell her perfume.

"I'm an independent bitch," she replied before looking him up and down and leaving.

This amazed Millertime and he couldn't wait to get his car and catch up to her. While driving down the track, he caught a glimpse of her apple ass and dark, luscious legs strolling with a purpose to serve him. Millertime stopped and said, "Damn, baby, don't walk too fast. Slow down so this moment can last. I can turn a small one to a tall one. You need to get at a pimp who's strong. We can sign it on the dotted line Georgia time, baby."

It didn't take long before she jumped in his car and they drove to a local motel for the night. If he only knew that this would be his last ride. After a couple drinks and some cocaine, the mood was just right and he was anxious to have her.

"Hold on, baby, I've got a surprise. So keep your hands to yourself for right now. I've never met a man like you, Millertime; and if you're going to have me, then you'll have to share me with my girlfriend."

She retrieved her phone, dialed, and proceeded as if she was talking to her girl, though it was me. "Hello—hey; where are you? Okay perfect; meet me at the Motel 6 on Candler Road. I've got a three-way puzzle that I need help putting together. Is he strapped?" She repeated my question from the other line.

She looked down at him and began to unbuckle his pants before continuing our conversation. "Yeah, he's completely naked," she said before hanging up, and so did I.

When I hung up the phone a devilish grin appeared on my face as I jotted down the math. I took a long drag from my Newport 100 before I put it out in the ceramic ashtray that my sister made me years ago, back in school. I strapped up with my chrome-plated Desert Eagle with graphite carbon fiber grip, equipped with 24K gold appointments and .300-grain jacketed hollow points.

I hopped in my rental and mashed the gas through traffic with intentions to put enough holes in this nigga that you'd think his daddy was a glassmaker. I have to admit, I was somewhat excited about the whole situation in regards to taking another man's life. It was not a concern whatsoever. He was dead the minute he violated my sister. Millertime just didn't know when I was going to retire his number.

I didn't hesitate to continue with my mission, and the consequences were overlooked easily the more I thought about him getting away with murder. I parked, and once the coast was clear, I got out, adjusted my shirt and proceeded to approach the room. I knocked three times and my adrenaline excelled. My decoy answered the door and let me in before running past me. Her job was done and she'd earned her salary for the day.

Millertime walked out of the bathroom covered in a towel, still unaware of the situation that was about to be presented, until he saw me in the mirror that faced him. His reaction was a paralyzed expression. He dashed for the drawer and I shot twice, hitting him once in the abdomen area. He fell instantly on the bed and lay there bleeding and breathing hard, with his eyes pulsating from left to right as if in shock or confusion.

"You don't have to do this—wait . . . I know you. Don't I know you? Wait a minute!" he pleaded. He was speaking a language that I didn't understand at that time, and mercy had no place in my heart. I knelt down, looked him in the eyes, and reminded him of my sister.

"You thought you were going to get away with killing my sister, my blood, nigga? Look at me!" Millertime just lay there defenseless and dying while I assisted his homecoming by putting a pillow over his face, only to hear his last muffled words.

"No it's . . . Change, Change, Change."

Bang! Bang! I shot twice through the pillow to guarantee a closed casket. Wasting no time, I noticed a snub nose .38 in the drawer and retrieved it before hightailing it out of there; making it a point to discard everything that linked me to this malicious crime. O.J. Simpson might have left one, but I made sure I had both of my gloves!

Driving back home was the longest drive ever as I thought about what I'd just done. It's not the actual killing that's hard, but the process of finishing what you started, and being there to see the results of death opens your eyes to the harsh reality that we live in. That man didn't wake up this morning expecting to have his noodles blown out of his head. And my sister didn't expect her demise either. Life is a bitch and death is her husband.

If it weren't for the lights behind me, I probably would have run the light in front of me. I tried not to panic considering I was responsible for expiring the life of another. I pulled over, took a couple breathers, and let God take it from there. The officer approached my vehicle with his flashlight beaming from his left hand, and his right hand on his weapon. My window was up, but when I heard him tap it with the light, it was game time.

"Sir, were you aware that you were going fifty-five miles per hour in a thirty-five miles per hour zone?"

"No, I'm sorry, officer, I wasn't paying attention. I'm trying to get to my son's day care to avoid the late fee."

"So driving reckless is just as responsible? Can I see your license and registration, please?" I reached into my glove compartment and grabbed the registration, but chose not to hand him my license because of any warrants I may have. "Here's my registration, but I forgot my license at home this morning. This is just a terrible week for me. My name is Brilliant Williams."

The officer looked like a slacker and I hoped this was the end of his shift. I could definitely use a break. He left for about five minutes and it seemed like an eternity. I looked through my rearview mirror the whole time, and when he returned, I crossed everything except my balls for good luck.

"Can you please step out of the vehicle, Mr. Williams?"

"Sure, what's the problem?"

"You have a warrant that came back outstanding. It doesn't explain in detail, but we'll have to detain you until we clear this matter. Do you have anybody that you can call to drive your car home? If not, then we'll have to notify a towing company."

Damn, I picked the wrong time to use my brother as an alias. And I'd forgotten about Brilliant mentioning a legal issue before. I guess the joke was on me; but I surely wasn't laughing. I've been using his name since I was fourteen, and now I have an issue because he decided to run away from his problems. That nigga can't think past abracadabra!

I was so nervous that I could literally smell the funky county jail cell. The police officer asked to search me and I agreed. I was thinking about my next step before the officer felt something suspicious and asked me to empty the contents of my front right pocket. I didn't know what it was until I remembered the piece that I took from the room, courtesy of the deceased.

I was hauled to the station and held without bail; and when my prints came back along with the history of the weapon, I was assed-out like Prince Pants. It turned out the gun was used in a string of robberies, and I had no problem with taking that charge. I'll do a bid for robbery over life for murder any day.

I couldn't fight the case and took a plea deal. The first day was the worst; but after a couple months in, I was already broken in. It wasn't that different than dealing with niggas on the street for real. And I knew enough guys in prison that I had no worries.

During my incarceration I kept in touch with James, and he held me down. He kept me up-to-date with what was going on with the label and he wasn't just talking shit. See, James was a square type of dude with brains, but didn't have any street credibility to get a ghetto pass, and I was just what he needed.

I guess he'd seen great things in me and I appreciated him for that. Therefore, we went hand in hand. I got him in contact with the people he needed to know like security, a street team, and a few artists that helped generate a buzz for the company locally—everybody was eating. He was doing exceptionally well and saw to it that I wanted for nothing.

Three years into my sentence my mother passed, and needless to say, that was a devastating loss. I attended the funeral and it meant a lot to me, but it was hard knowing that I was going right back to the bullshit. I really did think that James and I should have been brothers. I really had love for this cat. When he visited me, I loved to hear him talk about the record label that we owned and the properties in which our company invested in. An empire was being built for me on the outside and I was a few hours away from a new life.

THE PRODUCT OF HATE

On my way up from splashing water on my face, my boy, String, interrupted my thoughts as he walked into my cell.

"What's up, ace? Who is that? Damn she's fine!"

"This release date is up, and that's Kerri Hilson, fam! That's all." He was looking at my issue of *J'adore* magazine. If it wasn't for that and my television, I probably wouldn't have made it. The deputy told me to pack my shit, and it was finally time to ride. "I can't wait to get the hell out of here," I said before greeting him with a shake.

"Congrats, man. It's about time one of us gets out of this place. Yeah, just get me something fly to ride in when I get out, man. Oh, and don't trust ya family, man. Never believe what you hear and only half of what you see out there," String said. I guess that was the best advice he could give, but I didn't expect anything else different from him.

"Damn, I never thought this day would come," I said, still in disbelief about my departure.

"So what's the first thing you gonna do when you get outta the joint?" String asked and I was happy to answer.

"Man, I'm getting into three things: a fine whip when I'm out; a liquor store and get a bottle; and some pussy when I'm in my crib." We both laughed

35

and I began to pack my belongings before the deputy came back.

"Yo, you a cool dude, Bobby; hopefully we'll get up when I get out and I can be apart of the family. You know you're going to need a killa on your team!" he said with a serious look. And I knew he would literally kill for me.

In order for you to understand String, you would have to know his past. When Xavier aka String, was ten years old, he was kidnapped for a ransom. His uncle was LB, a well-known police officer who wasn't particularly respected in his parts for his corruption. It ranged from extortion, robbery, murder, falsifying documents, and crime-scene obstruction to sodomizing a thirteen-year-old girl, then having her placed in a state facility to bury the secret.

He had to be dealt with, and what goes around comes around, but payback does skip a generation, and unfortunately, a ninety-pound lovable and charismatic kid named Xavier was the primary target.

Summer of 1997 in Decatur, Georgia was like a fantasy to most, but a nightmare to one. Plans were made for a kid whose only troubles were his relationship to a man who barely claimed him. Xavier had no idea how a day of torture could mold his criminal path.

LB was taking a nap when the kidnapper called his cell phone, and upon answering it, it didn't take long for them to realize who they were dealing with.

"I've got your nephew and if you want to ever see him again, you need to pay attention very closely. Do you understand?" the voice on the other end of the phone said.

This was nothing new to LB, he was a veteran and used to the illegitimate conditions of the life he chose. But this was different; a crime too close to home that had to be catered to. It was his nephew whose life depended on LB's cooperation.

"Who is this?" LB demanded. At first he thought it was a joke or that he was dealing with some real amateurs. They were surely asking for trouble messing with him.

"That's not important, you're going to pay me fifty-thousand dollars or your nephew is going to endure so much pain, he'll beg me to end his suffering. This is not a game so don't play with me. That's what the lottery is for."

This unexpected call enraged LB, and just when the kidnappers thought their work so far was a sure success, the game suddenly flipped, putting the hot potato back in their hands. If they only knew that LB had no conscious, they would have reconsidered their attempt to extort him.

His heart was so cold he didn't sweat, and he concealed more hate than multiple death-row inmates. His soul consisted of revenge, lust, and pernicious thoughts that flattered his ego. Naturally he could care less who lived or died, as long as he had air in his lungs and got a piece of the action.

In his world there were no friends, family or coworkers; there was only LB, and then the world, to whom shall serve him. Every decision he has ever made was to his benefit, even if it cost someone else their life, then so be it. Unfortunately, Xavier found himself being used as an instrument for money; the only paper on earth worth selling your soul for.

"Stop right there you piece of shit, I don't negotiate with terrorist, but I will tell you this, so put your thinking cap on. I have a batting average of .300 out here in these streets, and if you proceed with this you will never sleep peacefully again. I'm warning you now to take my advice and tell me where the boy is, and I won't peel you like an orange!" LB's voice spoke in a tone that shifted the kidnappers, as if he had no intent at all with complying to their demands.

LB continued, "Are you following me? Give me the address and I'll forget about all of this. Be a smart guy."

"Smart huh? Yeah, I think the smart thing for you to do is pay me the fucking money or this kid is gonna feel every inch of this steel. His future isn't looking to promising over here, pig, I'm going to tell you one more—" LB hung up the phone with total disregard for the child's safety.

The kidnappers called numerous times afterward and failed to contact him. When LB got off the phone he noticed a couple of missed calls from Xavier's mother. When he called her back he knew he couldn't explain to her that his nephew's life was in his hands, and he chose to reject a monetary exchange to save him. His heartless actions could be her every incentive to discontinue her own life, as her life was motherhood.

"They took my son! Oh my God I don't know what to do. God, help me. You've got to find them LB. You're the cop; go get my baby, please." She was frantic and longwinded with her frenzied expressions of deep concern.

LB couldn't help but listen to his sister's cry for help, and he tried to think of another option to retrieve his nephew, but he was missing the only thing that produces a case: the lead.

"Okay, okay, Barbara. I'm on my way over there, but give me a second to figure some things out. I'm sure these guys won't harm him. It's probably just a misunderstanding. Everything will be all right. Don't I always take care of things? I'll call when I'm on my way."

LB contemplated about giving the money to save the boy, and it wouldn't have been that hard of a decision to make if it wasn't for an important deal that was going down the following day. So in all actuality, both of their lives were on the line. LB's if he didn't have the money for the exchange or his nephew's, if he keeps it.

He checked his voice mail and was shocked to hear a bone-chilling message left by the kidnappers, but recorded by Xavier himself: *"Uncle LB, please pick up the phone. These guys are mean and I want to go home. They said that you have something that they want and I can't go home until they get it."*

The message made it clear that the boy was being told what to say. Xavier was clearly shaken and confused about the incident that was taking place. Before hanging up, the kidnappers ended the conversation with a few encouraging words: *"If you think I'm playing then try me tough guy! If I don't hear from you in an hour this kid will not have a bright future at all."*

The heartless kidnapper's plan seemed to be spoiling, and they found themselves empty-handed, most importantly, angered by the way LB disrespected their authority. The only available solution to appease their frustration so far, was to cause pain—no specific kind—just pain.

The same livid and very impatient men approached Xavier where he was being held an hour later, and after giving up on LB's courtesy call, they gagged and tied his nephew by the neck to an air conditioner unit in the basement. Xavier was playful and loved to initiate games, but was unprepared for what awaited him.

Left downstairs in yet another confined space, Xavier wished to hear his grandmother's soft voice. He longed to feel her embrace him with the two arms that Mother Nature gave her to hold him. But I guess that's why they call it a wish. That definitely wasn't the reality of the situation.

The doped-up kidnappers went downstairs with alcohol sweating from their pores. They were unable to finish what they'd started without some kind of substance to pacify their animal instinct. Xavier woke up to two men blowing weed smoke in his face. The large amount of THC consumed was unbearable for the little boy. He was being treated like a test dummy, and round one was trying to compare lungs between men with an everyday habit, to an inexperienced child.

After their quarter ounce of Kush made its way in all three of their systems, it was then time for fun and games. The men then proceeded to throw darts at Xavier, and even kept score. A leg equaled ten points, which increased value for their scoreboard and humor, after forcing him to stand and dodge the darts. An arm equaled fifteen points because it was a harder target, since they were always moving. The stomach, chest, and face equaled thirty points, because it was unbelievably entertaining to throw darts at a child and get away with it. And the private area was a bull's-eye because they were just evil for putting him through this traumatizing experience.

"Hey, man, turn the dryer on. I'm tired of hearing him cry. What is the point of putting a sock in his mouth if you can still hear the little nigga?"

one of the kidnappers said, and the other accomplice did what he was told.

Later, he was introduced to Demon and Grasshopper. Two full-blooded, red nosed grand champion pit bulls, whose only purpose was to take pain, but most importantly, inflict it. They were tied across the room from Xavier and the chain was extended long enough to be inches away from what seemed to be their appetizer. If dogs could talk, they would have probably suggested that the boy just shut up and take his mauling like a man.

He was without food or a change of clothes, and the basement reeked of feces, heat, and sweat. Words can't explain the torture that he went through. Just before the kidnappers decided to spare Xavier's life, one of them figured he would be a decent punching bag for his thirteen-year-old son.

He was barely recognizable when the authorities found him in a trunk the next day. Luckily, a neighbor heard a suspicious pounding coming from a beat-up Honda Accord LX in a field, which happened to be Xavier's tied hands banging the inside of the trunk. A good boy turned bad, with no way to object to what had been done to him. This left Xavier with no options. Even though he was barely hanging on physically and emotionally, LB still did nothing at all to help him mentally.

After contacting a few resources in the street, it wasn't long before he discovered who had tortured Xavier. And for some reason, he couldn't let them get away with what they had done. They had to go; and what LB hated most was a poor choice maker. They had the opportunity to reconcile by accepting LB's initial proposal. Unfortunately they didn't; they had to pay their debt for declining to comply with his suggestions.

A week into Xavier's recovery on a sunny afternoon, LB paid his distant nephew an unexpected visit that wasn't accepted too well by his mother in the beginning, but he managed to take him out for a breath of fresh air. Mildly covered with visible bruises, the naïve and undermined Xavier jumped in the front seat and immediately began tuning the radio. LB passed Xavier a soda and he bashfully accepted. It was the perfect opportunity for LB to break the ice with an apology for allowing such a horrible experience to happen to this boy. But in retrospect, a secret is a secret, and the only thing that mattered to him at that time was retribution.

"Slow down, son, before you get sick, and put your seat belt on." Xavier didn't necessarily look up to his uncle, but already learned from other family members that he wasn't the type of guy to agitate. Needless to say, he was a little frightened and chose to take his mother's advice by doing more listening than talking. "You're tough, kid, you know that?" LB said as he readjusted his mirror before driving away.

"Mom says God saved me because I'm special, and I should pray for them," Xavier replied placing the half-empty can of soda into the cup holder.

LB looked at him for the first time since getting into the car. It was a look of disgust as if he were disappointed that his first reaction wasn't related to anger. Whatever anger Xavier didn't have that satisfied LB's standard, was only minutes away from being implemented.

"Do you think they prayed for you, boy? And God; where was he last week when you were being hurt, huh?"

"Where were you?" Xavier said in pain. His eyes looked a vacancy short of a soul, and easily became influenced by his uncle's selfless words. Because of their common interest in self-loathing and disfavor, he became vulnerable. With an itch that needed to be scratched that was obviously the taste for revenge to be the authority and not the victim; that's all that LB could offer as an uncle; the naked truth.

Surprised by Xavier's remark he became tense and exhaled a breath of words that changed Xavier's life forever, "You're not my responsibility, boy. You take to your mother's side of the family; a bunch of homo's and underachievers who pile up in one house and still can't manage to pay the rent. And your mother tells you to pray? No, you go out there and inflict the same pain, if not more, on their asses!"

LB merged onto the freeway as he received a text message. Xavier sat motionless in the passenger seat with a cynical looking grin. He was losing his grip inside.

"I guess you want to know where we're going. Well it isn't Disneyland! It's time for you to sample a taste of a little thing called power."

Xavier's heart began to beat a thousand miles per second, and his head began to pulsate feverishly. His head was forced back as LB excelled the vehicle before slowing his speed a half of mile further. They followed closely behind a black van on I-85; a van that Xavier refers to now as the murder wagon. Xavier had no idea what was going on until his uncle explained everything to him.

LB cleared his throat and firmly said, "Okay, Xavier, do you see that van in front of us? There are some bad people in that van that I need you to identify for me."—He winked before continuing—"Do you think you can do that for me, or do you want to go back home and pray for these guys to do what they did to you to someone else?"

Having an idea who his uncle was talking about, he agreed.

LB got on the phone and signaled the drivers in the van ahead of him the green light to proceed with the premeditated plan. When he got off the phone, the van doors opened and two men were almost out of the van hanging by their shirts with there hands bound, mouths taped, and gangsters behind them. It was broad daylight and traffic was a nightmare. Cars and eighteen-wheelers were speeding to get to their locations.

LB looked at Xavier and asked with a deep voice, "Are those the guys that kidnapped you?" Xavier couldn't get a good view, so his uncle drove closer to the side of the van.

When Xavier got a clear view of the men, he looked with fear and retaliation while shaking his head. LB put his window down to give the signal before they reduced speed and merged to the left lane. The kidnappers were thrown from the van and Xavier was forced to watch the whole decapitation take place. Body parts were everywhere and it was a gruesome scene to witness. Yet, a sense of satisfaction engulfed the young boy's psyche.

A killer was created that day and he hasn't been right since then. String has been state property since he was twelve. His problems began with fights that graduated him to being a bully, and later transitioned him and enhanced his attitude as gang-sta. Always graduating to higher levels of crime, he didn't take no for an answer and had no qualms about doing jail time.

Standing on the thresholds of another incarceration stint, String took his eight-year sentence for attempted murder; his third felony with a smile. He argued in court about the injustice of his hood and debated with the judge throughout the trial.

"Mr. Davis, please compose yourself. You're in a court of law and you can't act this way if you want a lesser sentence," his lawyer whispered.

"Go to hell, man! You're a public defender who gets paid when I'm found guilty and hauled to the side in chains. This system is a joke, so just take me to jail! Who would ever regret putting a woman beater in his place? No woman deserves to be treated like trash; especially my sister. And I'll be excited to find out if her ex didn't wake up from his coma," String busted out with his last words.

The judge calmly looked at him and said, "I am also a man with principles and would go berserk if a single hand touched my mother, sister or wife, without their permission to do so. However, in the state of Georgia your reaction to protect your sister is unlawful, and beating a man half to death is punishable up to fifteen years in prison.

"But the details surrounding the event did pose the victim, Mr. Bradshaw, as a threat, and he was no angel. But what you did was against the law, and for that, I hereby sentence you to eight consecutive years in the Atlanta State Penitentiary.

"We'll see how good you make on your debt to society. Hopefully, you'll experience reform and one day become a tax paying citizen; bailiff, please take the prisoner."

The judge was pretty harsh to say the least, but with his priors, he's lucky the he didn't throw the book at him. He's told me over and over again about that day and how all he could hear in his head is the comment that the judge made about him becoming a tax paying citizen. I mean, he really wanted to change.

We are all products of our past and without guidance, incidents like Xavier's, whether big or small, can shape your future. In my six years of incarceration, I've met a lot of good and bad men, to say the least, but judging a man by circumstance is a terrible habit. Just opening my ears to a man's testimony helped me understand the transition between a boy and a man, inside and outside, real and fake, and in this case, Xavier turning into String.

To society, he is a criminal, but to me he is a friend. String was asking countless questions about my belongings, and if he only waited for me to finish with what I was doing, he wouldn't have had to try so hard to persuade me to leave him my things.

"What's mine is yours," I replied, throwing my *J'adore* magazine at him. "It's nothing, man." The deputy walked up shortly after and for once, I felt like he worked for me as he was ordered to escort me out of there.

"Mr. Williams, let's go. It's time to checkout," the deputy said after interrupting String and I.

Finally, this was the last day I'd use a pay phone, see these bars, deal with the overcrowding, or live on a bunk surrounded around unhygienic materials within these claustrophobic walls. Worst of all: hearing grown men cry at night and COs using attack dogs for cell extractions, and that's just a portion of my problems with the prison system. And the next time I sleep alone is going to be by choice. I feel like I made it and was eager to get out and live a productive and honest lifestyle.

After processing out of their system, the corrections officer escorted me through those nasty coarse gates. I heard a buzz, and like that, I was leaving with the same clothes on that I came from court in, with a manila envelope full of paperwork and an agenda to live my kinda life.

THE RELEASE

"What up, my nigga? Wanna go to the clinic? I know you been fucking with those boys." He laughed.

My eyes squinted; not because I didn't recognize the voice, but because the sun was just as happy to see me. James was standing in front of a silver 2009 BMW 7 series, looking fly to death, like he was worth some millions. I embraced my brother from another mother, and we got in the car.

As James drove, I couldn't stop looking at my past through the rearview mirror. I quickly snapped out of it before James had to tell me about our plans for the night. He gave me a small jewelry box that he called a starter kit. Once I opened the box I knew we were in the big leagues. It contained an American Express blue card, an iced-out company medallion with ideal cut emerald and white gold diamonds, an iPhone, two sets of keys, and an appointment reminder. I asked about the appointment and he jokingly told me that I needed lessons to drive my Honda CBR600RR. Now that's a real homie for you.

People these days keep company around them they know they shouldn't keep. Loser types with no goals, just waiting on someone in their camp to come up so they can bum a free ride. I made it a priority to stay away from niggas who wore them long red shoes. Clowns had no place in my social circle. I had a lot on my mind and needed some closure, so I told James to take me to Rest Haven Gardens Cemetery, where my mother was buried. We stopped at a local flower shop and I picked up some roses. I bought one for every year that I missed.

"Hey, mom, sorry that we're meeting again under these circumstances, but I guess in a positive light, we're both free. I'm gonna do right now, momma, and I need you to continue to look over me. When I was in that place, I heard your voice all the time, and I knew that you were watching over me.

"In the streets I had everything that I felt I needed at that time, the hoes, clothes, and pretty payrolls, but deep down I was missing something. There was a gap in my life and the bridge was feeling wanted. I guess I was searching for love, but all I had to do was come back home.

"I took advantage of your presence because it was convenient. I miss you looking at me, giving me tips on how to treat a woman, and correcting my English. I miss the small things, but I will always remember them and I'll always remember you." I kissed her tombstone, before I hopped back in the car.

When I got in, James was on the phone with an unpleasant look. I could tell whomever he was talking to was telling him something he didn't want to hear. I tried to ignore the issue but I felt tension, so out of concern I asked James about any problems that he might be dealing with. He didn't acknowledge my question and quickly changed the subject.

Then James said, "I don't think I could have seen you in those fucking walls another year, my nigga. I'm happy to see you. Much has changed since you've been in. Of course, our tax bracket, and I definitely ain't complaining about that, but it's a new ball game; we're on a whole new level now. I stepped on some toes to get where I'm at, and all I'm saying is that we need to be careful of those around us."

I listened carefully to everything James told me. He went on to tell me that he wanted me to manage most of our properties personally, because of a fallout that he'd had with someone who he thought he could trust. Money isn't the root of all evil; it's only when you let it control you when it begins to destroy every beneficial feature in your life.

We owned office buildings in Atlanta along with some rehab houses in surrounding areas, and two beauty salons near the downtown business district, and urban neighborhood. James was very smart and knew that as long as he owned his property, he could attain his wealth through lucrative investments to compass a legitimate future uninterrupted due to his assets.

We stopped at the Mall of Georgia and picked up some gear; something small just to hold me over for a couple of days. A couple of outfits were straight and besides, my stomach was touching my back. It's like the ladies could smell my new money, and this was something not necessarily new to me, but my swagger was different, and it wasn't too long until I noticed that I was *that* nigga. James let me enjoy my shine as I pulled some dimes. I mean 6' 1", 200 pounds, with a caramel complexion, straight teeth and a fresh cut; shit, I was killing them.

We left the mall and James told me to drive. I didn't even want to do that much talking; just drive and feel the breeze, and recollect my transition from ex-convict to operating manager for Good Game Records.

"Damn, this dude is nice; who is this?" I asked and James smiled while turning up the radio and knodding his head.

"That's our new artist Vgo D'artiste. He's our ticket to the big leagues. He's got the image, style, and vocals to go commercial. He's already turned down a major deal, but we're talking and I think we got him."

"Man, we gotta sign this dude and he doesn't even sound like he's from here." Just looking at the changes in the area since my incarceration amazed me, and I loved it.

I felt like driving all night even though I didn't have a license, and if I were pulled over, I'd probably be better off using my name this time in oppose to my brother's anyway. James was on the phone and I couldn't help but notice the new development since I've been gone. Everybody just seemed to be in a rush, but not me. I took my time to enjoy every minute of my day.

"Yeah, you know what time it is; and don't I always take care of you? Yeah, you and that chocolate thing would be just fine. Yeah, about nine sharp. Talk to you later."

"Who was that?" I asked.

"Oh, just some chicks that are trying to get on, that's all."

"So they sing or what?"

"Oh yeah, they can blow, they'll be over here later for an audition, so you can see for yourself," he said while extending his arm giving me directions. We were in a residential area that looked prominent, and it was definitely something that I wasn't used to.

"What's here?"

"Man, will you stop asking so many questions and just come on—damn. You done went to jail a smooth talking hustler and came out acting like a nosy neighbor!" James said sarcastically.

"Shut up, chump." We got out and walked up to a two-story house.

"Hey, we'll be here for a minute, I know your hungry or something, but I just have to handle something real fast."

It was obvious to me that whoever stayed here had appealing taste. We found ourselves outside of this house and I was waiting for James to ring the doorbell, or something.

"Damn, nigga, are we just going to stand here?" I said.

"I'm waiting on you," James replied.

"For what; to pick the lock? My first day out and you want me to do a job with you. What type of shit are you on?" I asked.

"This is your house, not mine. I live in a condo, so open the door with your punk ass!" James said.

I remembered the set of keys that he gave me, and after a few attempts I found the right key and it unlocked the door. I took my time walking in before I heard . . . "SURPRISE!" I almost pissed my pants when I saw all my loved ones at my welcome home party, in my new home.

As I looked with disbelief, I couldn't imagine all the people who actually cared for me. I definitely didn't see this one coming. Everybody I knew was there except Brilliant, he was in Iraq on his second tour. Luckily he resolved his issue with the courts, and it wasn't serious enough to prevent him from enlisting. James's mother must have cooked everything but oodles and noodles, and I enjoyed every minute of it. It's funny how you reminisce your childhood when you're amongst friends.

It brings back memories; memories so clear that you can pinpoint society's corruption targeting the urban inner-city youth in America. But even though we all go through our trial and tribulations, I lived for moments like these; the dominoes slamming and card shuffling, friendly debates, and eating off paper plates. I couldn't have asked for a better welcome home party. I just wish Momma and Pamela were here.

Everything started to wind down around ten that night and it was time to enjoy the nightlife. I had to get dressed and needed to freshen up. James fell on the couch and took a deep breath before looking at his phone. The party was over and the house was empty.

"What happened to the audition; the chicks cancelled?" I asked.

"I told them to come around ten. I didn't plan on things ending so quickly. Anyway, I gotta go to the house and get dressed, so meet me at my house and we'll leave for the club together. If anything comes up just holla. My address is saved in your car," he said getting up from the couch and stretching.

"All right, well give me forty minutes and I'll be over."

"I doubt that; oh, and nice car!" he said pointing at my matching seven series in the driveway.

"Thanks, I have good friends," I said humorously.

He hopped in his car, drove off, and the beat in his car excited me. I practically ran upstairs to get ready. I couldn't believe how my day was going. I felt so good, I had a smile so wide on my face that I could have ate a banana sideways. Bobby Williams was back and I could honestly say that I was what I inspired to be six years ago, which proved to me, if you think it, you can achieve it.

Shit, six years using state soap, I was excited to even smell Irish Spring. I giggled to myself thinking how long it's been since I've actually taken a shower without having sandals on.

"Hello? Hey, James!" I yelled after opening the shower door. I could have sworn that I heard some noise downstairs. I was probably just hearing things so I continued singing, *"I had a dream I could buy my way to heaven; when I awoke I spent that on a necklace; I told God I'd be back in a second; Man it's so hard not to be reckless. . . . Wait till I get my money right. . . ."*

I feel like Kanye is talking to me whenever I hear that song. I heard another noise and it interrupted my zone. I decided to go and see what was going on, and a continuous knock at the door let me know that my speculations were true. I knew that I wasn't going crazy. James must have decided to come back instead of me driving to him.

"Yo, nigga, why you aint just . . ." I said while opening the door, still wet with only a towel.

"We're here for the audition, are you Bobby?"

Two of the sexiest women I've ever seen were at my door as if I were the solution to their problems. James is a sneaky dude and I couldn't help but laugh thinking about his comment about calling him if something came up, so I did.

"Hey, man, something came up!" I said when he picked up the phone.

"Welcome home, man. Just meet me at the club when you're finished. You can't help but notice us when you get there. And where a rubber, boy!" he said jokingly.

"I always do, bro." I hung up the phone before showing the ladies my southern hospitality. They entered the room and I couldn't stop looking at them. We instantly became glued to each other and I couldn't keep my hands off of them.

The first girl was white with blue eyes, long curly hair, silicone tits, and a slim face, with long legs that I pictured wrapped around me, and a walk that can cure the sick.

"What's your name, sexy?" I asked.

"Tuesday," she said.

She looked unpredictable, and I had to admit it turned me on. The other chic was straight out of a rap video. She had to be 5' 8" tall, and slim, with a nice ass, hazel eyes, with a ponytail and dark complexion that fit her perfectly.

"And I'm Coco," she said. My dick immediately got hard, stretching my towel and causing it to untangle.

Both women were half-dressed in lingerie with gaps that complimented their frames. They escorted me to my king-sized bed, and I fell back on the pillow top mattress. They followed, surrounding me from both sides with kisses and an adequate approach to giving. Both were experienced in the field of sexual pleasure, and I couldn't wait to bring the best out of them.

Tuesday grabbed my mushroom as it inflated in her hand. She wasted no time showing me her oral capabilities, while Coco encouraged my exploration of her smooth body.

Intimacy is a state of mind if you ask me, or could even be explained as a desired occupation between lovers, but that wasn't the case here. I just wanted to beat that pussy up like it snitched on me, and take a detour in their freaky-fuck tunnel.

These beauties were at my disposal and I definitely took advantage of it. We were all over each other, and you'd think it was their first day out too! They looked so edible, and even though I'd just met them, I chose not to minimize the value in my fantasy.

"Damn, baby, suck it harder and use a lot of spit; there you go." Tuesday's mouth played the soundtrack to our sexplosion, and set the tone for me to reciprocate. Coco was licking my chest and working her way to my neck, before I grabbed her by her hair and kissed her. Her lips were so soft that they gave her words more value. She bit my lip and it never felt so good.

"Get up and face the headboard, boo. I want you to ride this handsome face." She did as she was told, and she danced to her own beat as my hands palmed her ass, attempting to impress her enough to always remain a memory in her best sex category.

Her scent was driving me crazy, and sucking on her clit caused her to vibrate. I played with her though. I'm an expert at eating pussy, but I didn't want to give her too much. It might just take a psychologist to get me out of her head. Tuesday took it upon herself to ride me reverse cowgirl, and I can tell she was a screamer and liked it rough.

"Yeah, right there, baby, bounce on it—damn."

"How's my pussy taste, Bobby?" Coco asked as if she needed a review.

"Yeah, Bobby, how's the audition going?" Tuesday added. She got off me and began to rub, kiss and tease Coco, which made great for a transition.

"I'd rather watch ya'll together than television any day. Show me what you two are capable of doing if men didn't exist."

They toppled each other and were creating art right before my eyes. I was turned on, and if women knew how much that turned a man on, they'd probably consider bringing it to the bedroom regularly. I smacked her ass while I jerked myself to keep it hard, and I swear it grew another inch just looking at them.

"Put it in and stop playing, daddy. Come and be apart of this party in my pussy," Coco said, and she didn't have to say it twice. I grabbed the magnum and ripped it open. I stood up on the floor and opened that ass wide to make sure every inch of my dick felt the warmth of her southern hospitality. She was so wet it sounded like I was smacking water.

"Harder, Bobby, harder . . . mmm," Coco said. The sex was so good that she had to stop tasting Tuesday to take a second to look at me. Tuesday grabbed her head to continue and Coco moaned hysterically while using her arms to open her ass wide for me. I was about to cum so I slowed down. I wanted to celebrate a holiday on Tuesday's calendar.

"Hey, both of you lay down right here for me," I insisted; and they propped themselves with their legs open, and they were available to me like government assistance. I threw Tuesday's legs over my shoulder and gripped her breast before penetrating her with my best. The energy in the air was spectacular, and history was maybe taking place. With all the sexual animosity about to be released, I began to finger Coco faster and faster.

"Don't stop." She began to grind hard and squeeze her breast. She screamed in satisfaction and couldn't contain herself. I was turned on by it and pulled out seconds later.

"Take it off, baby, I wanna feel that cum," Tuesday said. She rushed up and began to give me head until she was sucking the life out of me. This experience is just what I needed, and if I got the death penalty right now, I'd die a happy man.

"I don't know what to say, ladies; thanks," I said smiling from ear to ear. I reached over to get my phone from my pants pocket and threw it to Coco. I liked her the most.

"Here, put your number in my phone. I'm about to take a shower and ya'll can join if you'd like. I've gotta be out of here right after." They agreed and truthfully, I was excited to get out and to the club.

"Hey, welcome back, I hope we were fun, and I hope we can have another audition someday for another role or something, ya know?" Coco said before they left.

"Oh yeah, I like y'all's style; and don't trip, I'ma call you. Lock the door behind you on the way out though, babe."

"Gotcha, daddy."

"Bye, Bobby. It was a pleasure," Tuesday said on her way out behind Coco.

I opened my bag and popped the tags on my new outfit before I walked downstairs and took a short detailed tour of my new house. Still overwhelmed with my blessings, I recognized very well that James spoiled me more in one day, than I've been in my whole life. Being alone gave me the opportunity to talk to the Father and give grace for my blessings.

"Lord, thank you for the air that I breathe and the bread that I eat. Without You, I'll surely be lost and confused like a dog gone astray. Continue to lead me in the right direction, as I will try my best to make elite decisions for a better future. God is love, Amen."

I took two shots of Hennessy and popped my collar before I bounced to the Black Cherry, a familiar club that I'm used to. The smell of fresh leather made me feel brand new as I adjusted my windows and seats to fit my level of comfort. I could smell myself, and Sean John's cologne really made me feel like a king, and every man should have a similar scent with no exceptions. I turned the ignition and Al Green was talking to me through my Alpine speakers.

"I'll get along, I'm sure you'll find another. Baby, please remember . . . I'll be here . . . I'm gonna stay right here . . . if you should ever find to need me."

For the good times is my shit. And yeah, I was feeling nice and highly anticipating my entrance to the club; ready to recapture the true essence of hood star treatment.

The sound of my alarm caused a few heads to turn, but everything about me represented power. I walked across the street in my white, blue, and red Key's collared T-shirt, with matching jeans and Prada shoes. I immediately noticed that the club was poppin', and I just couldn't wait to get in there. I approached the bouncer, and to my surprise, we knew each other.

"What's up, Bobby! Man, I heard you just got out and you already doing good. I'm trying to get on your level, huh!" He looked around before continuing, "So who did you come with; by yourself? You want to get bottle service? Because I'll set you up with a nice table . . ."

I stopped him from wasting his breath. He must have thought I was a general admission type of dude, so I had to let him know.

"Nah, I'm not buying any tables tonight, they're already paid for. I'm with James Fullerton."

"Oh, so you rolling with the big dogs now; huh, shawty? Let him in, he's VIP." Another bouncer opened the rope for me to enter, and once I got in the club, I stopped to take everything in, thinking, *The king has arrived.*

Heading toward the VIP section, I walked through the crowd making friendly gestures like I owned the club, until I observed James socializing with some gentlemen. Young Jeezy was playing and everybody was going nuts. Man, the frequencies in his music made you want to cop an eight ball and get on that block for that money!

"It's about time, Bobby. I was starting to get worried about you. How did you like the surprise?" James said.

"Ain't no limit to your surprises, homie. Next thing you're going to tell me is that this is your club," I said.

James laughed then and said, "Well, it's funny you mentioned that. Gentlemen, this is my friend and fifty-fifty partner, Bobby Williams. And Bobby, these were the owners of this fine establishment."

"Congratulations. You're lucky to have such an honest businessman by your side. Guys like James are hard to come by. Well our business is done and, James, if you know a decent entertainment lawyer, then throw me a bone, I can surely use one."

"I'll have my guy give you a call in the morning. He's the best," James confidently responded.

"Nice to meet you, gentlemen," I said before shaking their hands. The men walked away leaving James and I to toast to life, amongst other things.

"Hey, man, this is only the beginning. The last six years of your life has been hell, but the next six, my friend, will make your sacrifice well worth it. You're my guy."

It was loud in the club but James's words were so clear to me, and it felt so good knowing that through all the troubles and the losses we go through in life, all it takes is that one; and I'm blessed to have that.

"You know how much your sister loved clubs, shit, that's where I met her crazy ass!"

"Yeah, she did love to dance," I said before continuing, "Remember her nickname?" I asked with a chuckle reminiscing about Pam.

"How can I forget, rain was her favorite element, and mine as well. Money reminds me of money," James said before taking a sip of his Rosé.

"How about we call it . . ."

"Element!" we both said together.

"We're going to change the name to Element. I can see it now: ELEMENT," James said, opening his arms as if he were spelling the name.

A SOUL SOLD FOR A BIT OF CONTROL

In six years, James put a plan into action and executed it wonderfully. I was proud to realize that we were bosses. But there were a couple of questions that I had to find out like: whose toes were stepped on to get where we were now, and were we one hundred percent legitimate?

Before I was able to ask them, James poured us a glass of Rosé before escorting me into a private room and explaining a few details; or at least what he thought I needed to know now until further notice. He owned up to the fact that there were no records to prove his income during the time investments were made for the company, and it drew the attention of numerous local law enforcement officers, one in particular, who went by the name of Lonnie Biggs.

From my understanding, they had a good relationship at one time; James used him to enforce his intricate network of schemes from robberies and home invasion, to guarding after-hour parties and any other monetary opportunity to exploit Lonnie Biggs's authority. James knew the resources and Lonnie Biggs had the muscle. But unsuspecting to his agenda, Lonnie Biggs let his guard down; something he usually didn't do.

Their relationship collapsed after Lonnie introduced James to a well-established businessman with an interest in investing for a quick return. It was a great opportunity for James, considering his energy was focused on improving his record label and realty company.

His attachment to Lonnie Biggs backfired due to Lonnie's reputation, and it was bad business. Before he decided to cut him off though, he came up with a scam that he learned from his Nigerian friend; a scam not too expensive to produce, and the payout was just what he needed to get his personal business off the ground and pursue bigger ventures. He was too smart for his own good, but too dumb to think it wouldn't catch up to him one day.

Lonnie Biggs vouched for James; which intrigued this businessman from New York, and he soon became interested in how he could double his investment in ninety days. A meeting was scheduled and the investor flew to Atlanta, where James had the opportunity to pitch his elaborate money machine.

"Victor Mansfield, this is James Fullerton, the gentleman I spoke to you about. Now let's get to business, shall we?" Lonnie Biggs said as they sat down and got comfortable.

"So, Lonnie says you're an expert in turning nothing into something. From my understanding, you possess a device that can print US currency; is that correct?" Victor asked. He wouldn't take his eyes off of him, and as greedy as he was, James really had to sell this scam in order for it to work.

"That's true, my device can duplicate money, and not just American currency, but foreign notes as well. It's fairly simple, Mr. Mansfield. Once the image is scanned, and then downloaded to the memory in this device, it will print the exact image with every detail. However you choose to wash your money is on you. But if you want this machine, you'd have to pay me the manufacturing cost and a fee for the paper, which is a total of seventy-five thousand."

"Interesting; so when can I see this magical device of yours?" Victor asked while rubbing his hands together.

"It's right here, actually. And I want to demonstrate the genius of its continuity." James then pulled it out of a laptop bag and pressed the activate button. Victor looked in awe as the sound of the device powering up intrigued him. But what he didn't know was that James had placed a real hundred-dollar bill in the machine prior to the meeting, and the machine was just as useless as a three-dollar bill. The device printed a single bill in ten minutes, and Victor looked at Lonnie Biggs with a look that confirmed his interest.

"There are one hundred sheets of paper in here already. That's all it would hold," James said while opening it for them to view for themselves.

"What the hell. I've never seen anything like that in my life!" Lonnie Biggs said.

"Hmm." Victor was shocked, and Lonnie's reaction influenced his greed.

"Well my dad told me during my junior year in college to never sleep on a winner, and as convinced as I am, I'm going to need you to impress me a little bit more than that," Victor said as a plea for enough satisfaction to give James his money. James called the waitress and gave the money to her, along with the bill, and they all watched her walk to her station with it.

"Oh, and don't worry, guys, drinks are on me tonight," James said with a grin that confirmed his big payday. He glanced at Lonnie Biggs and wondered if he was about to fuck the wrong person, but to him this was a necessary sacrifice. He knew that Lonnie Biggs was a ruthless guy, but James was up and coming and definitely wasn't going to let a washed-up detective come between him and his new order.

"If this waitress comes back with change, I'm going to sleep good tonight," Victor said.

"Well if she doesn't, then you've got the bill; I know that!" James said and the two laughed.

The waitress came back. "Here's your change."

"No, you keep it, hun. Thanks," James replied.

Lonnie and Victor were sure they found the answer to all of their problems. They walked out to discuss the next day's transaction.

"Well, I'm only in town until tomorrow night, but we can meet around noon at my house; which is great because I can kill two birds with one stone, and pack my clothes as well. And I suggest you bring cash. I don't accept checks,"

James said and everyone laughed aloud. Lonnie and Victor liked James and wondered where this guy came from.

"Seventy-five thousand doesn't sound too bad. I think I can handle that. Lonnie told you who I was, right?"

"I'm aware that you're all about your business, and that's why I inquired about you. And I assure that you're making a good decision. In fact, my machine will speak for itself. The only downside to my device is it only prints every two hours, but holds enough ink to produce for six months, which will print twelve bills a day totaling thirty-six thousand a month. In six months, if you print consistently, you're going to make good on your return; an exceptional two hundred sixteen thousand dollars."

"Have you ever been to the Big Apple, James?" Victor said to James opening his car door.

"Only on business, but I never got the opportunity to spread my wings," James replied.

"Well next time you're in town, you've got to stop by my estate in The Hamptons. Just keep impressing me, kid, and I'll make you a very rich man. Lonnie, give him my number; and I guess I'll see you guys tomorrow morning."

The meeting was arranged for noon the next day, but the location that was supposed to be James's house, wasn't. The next day went as planned, and they met James in his parking lot.

"Hey, James; beautiful day, isn't it? So you're going out of town on business?" Victor said, holding a Burberry messenger bag.

"I have a family reunion in Detroit, and when you're paying for everything, you at least want to get there on time, right?"

"Absolutely!" Victor said laughing aloud.

"Is that the money in that expensive looking bag?" James asked humorously.

"Well I make good on my promises and been around for quite a while, and in six months, I want to help you sell these things; you follow me?"

"I'm right behind you. Here, you can give me that."

James took the bag and opened his trunk where the device was. He grabbed it and handed it to Lonnie Biggs. But when he slammed the trunk, he noticed a nosy neighbor looking suspiciously at him. He began to get a little uncomfortable, and knew he had to get things solidified. After all, it wasn't his property.

"Gentlemen, it was nice doing business with ya; and Lonnie, I'll see you when I get back," James said in an attempt to speed up things.

"Hey, just a second; you know last night amazed me, and I have to see that magic again before I get on this flight."

Lonnie and Victor were acting funny as if they were aware of the scam, and were persistent in activating the device in front of James again. Victor brought it to his car and activated it, and it was a very tense moment.

"I can't wait any longer, fellas. I've got many things to do."

"It's just ten minutes, James, come on! Don't be a diva. It would make me feel a whole lot better if you stayed," Lonnie said and James did just that, knowing that if the police were called it would only stall everything. Five minutes later when the bill showed, he smiled. Knowing that a smart man would have requested to do the same, James refilled it that morning.

"We're in business! Grab it; let's go, Lonnie."

Victor shook James's hand and Lonnie stayed back until Victor got in the car.

"So where's my ten percent?" Lonnie inquired.

"Meet me at the café at three." When they left, James left and never spoke to them again. So now whose toes are swollen?

James's reaction to his own story let me know something distinctive about this Lonnie character. He was definitely someone to be taken seriously. I looked into James's eyes and saw another man; a man with secrets, a man with a life that superseded his expectations, a man who beat the system; my nigga!

Groupies were everywhere trying to be near us. It was amazing to see them fight nail and teeth to be noticed and exploited. The same chicks that wouldn't give a brotha play if he wasn't doing it big. That is when I knew that I was destined to be on top, because it was too crowded on the bottom. We must have left at three in the morning, and they wanted to eat, but I was tired so I went straight to the house.

When I woke up I called James, but he didn't answer, so I decided to get dressed and hit the barbershop on Decatur Road. I didn't really need a cut but stuck around anyway to holla at my homies. I heard everything that went on while I was in that place. I didn't even bother to ask why none of them came to see me. Like my sister used to say, it's just a part of the game.

Man, this shit was crazy. Being locked down institutionalized me. I mean, everyday for six years I had a pattern and adjusted to it, and now I could do whatever I wanted with my time. Right when I was thinking about my next step, James called me to meet him at the office on Peachtree Street.

When I got there, it felt like my first day at work. James laid down some rules before issuing me a personal security guard to keep me company. He also advised me to acquaint myself with the properties we owned, along with the tenants who occupied them. Once I made my presence known and everyone knew whom to report to, we headed to a location for a video shoot.

Vgo D'artiste was an artist on our label and he was a real nigga, as hard as the concrete we walk on. I could tell he was going places, and it's strange because I have never heard of him before until then. I assumed that he had to have been from another state, but he told me that he was from Stone Mountain, but caught a charge in Virginia and did a three-year bid out there. One scene in the video was supposed to portray him as the creator of woman, and it was titled "Diva Chick." Now it's my national anthem.

Business went on as usual and I wouldn't trade my life for anybody's. It took me close to two months to learn the ins and outs of my responsibilities as partner of Good Game Records and JB Realty. It was harder than I expected to make a transition as big as the one I made.

My first two months out and in the blink of eye, I came from sleeping on a bunk to pressing a foreign emblem to open my trunk. I'm used to putting in my own work, and now I had killers on the payroll that wouldn't let you get close enough to smell my cologne. James, on the other hand, wanted it all: the red carpet treatment and idolized John Gotti, and I just preferred to stay away from the light like Sam Giancanna. We debated about this on numerous occasions.

For some reason, I feel more comfortable living a regular life, and don't mind going back to the hood. You see, extortion wasn't an issue that I ever had to deal with, due to the simple fact that I was respected, and I was known for playing fair in the field of opportunity.

"Nigga, you crazy," James said.

"I learned a lot from MC Hammer."

James laughed. "What's that?"

"A nigga can't save the whole hood, but you can put a couple of my homies on, so they can eat."

"True, true."

"In my experience, dealing with diversified crowds and social groups, I've learned that a high percentage of inner-city dwellers like myself, wouldn't live long enough to enjoy the luxury of change."

"That's because opportunities for most of us are categorized, and the majority leads to a prison number," James said.

"Man, I went and tried to get a few of them dudes to distribute flyers and do some street, teamwork and everyone of them had an excuse— or something like that!"

"Simple, them niggas ain't wanting to work!" James shouted before continuing, "You can't save the world. Just live your life because it's short, man."

James only wanted the best to work for me, and didn't qualify anyone for a position who didn't deserve it. He was all about business and our progress was evidence of that. We finally signed Vgo D'artiste, and when I say it was a blessing to have good talent, I really meant it. With our affiliates at Nason Mathias Marketing Firm, a platinum record was soon to come. We also had an R&B singer named Sydne Renee. She made a name for herself in the Atlanta area and luckily we signed her, because it wasn't long before a label got to her. We only signed the best and were even lenient with their contracts. They toured a lot, and sometimes I tagged along to make sure things went smoothly, even though we had people for that.

Vgo D'artiste was our golden egg and he understood the game quite well. I remember him guaranteeing me a double-platinum album, and on our way back from Florida, James told me he had someone for me to meet. Knowing him and his surprises, I was expecting the president.

He promised me that everything was going to be fine when I got locked up. True to his word, everything was fine. I've heard so many people promise me shit in these streets and I tried to believe the good in their word, but good intentions are the mother of all fuck-ups. Satisfyingly, James came through and for that, I'd lay my life for him.

I woke up to my doorbell ringing, and it was a constant and annoying sound. I practically ran downstairs, still dizzy from jumping out of the bed. When I opened the door, it was James rushing me to get dressed. Just when I was about to decline his invitation to lunch, he signaled someone in the car to get out. The door opened and I saw what appeared to be a detailed description of a page out of a romantic novel in the physical form. There was something about the woman that did something to me, and she had not even spoken yet.

As she walked towards us I became complacent. An inadvertent tingle played with my heart as my brain raced for the perfect words to brand my everlasting impression. Since my release, I haven't seen James with a woman, and I think this is why. Just thinking about the angels who were paid time-and-a-half to work overtime for the creation of this woman, was an addition to my prayers. She had to be 5' 6" tall with long, straight hair, perfect golden complexion, C-cup natural breasts that sat high enough to deny gravity, a flat stomach that would put Janet Jackson to shame, and not to mention, an ass that fit her body so well. As long as I had a face, she'll always have a place to sit. She was dynamic from head-to-toe, and I just needed to search her mind and body to discover her flaws.

"This is Jennifer; and Jennifer, this is Bobby," James said.

She gave me hug and I got weak as I embraced her healthy vibe, while our bodies exhaled together. She took a step back before placing her hands on my shoulders and interrupting James's introduction.

"Bobby! Oh, I've heard so much about you, and it's nice to finally see you in person. James speaks highly of you, and now I know why. I can't even tell the difference between you two by looking in your eyes. They are almost identical. He even asked me to come and visit, but I figured these would be better circumstances," Jennifer spoke softly.

Then James jumped in, "And besides, I wanted to surprise you, man. Three years for a surprise seems long, but she changed me. We're getting married and I'm going to spend the rest of my life with her."

That's when I smiled and said, "Congratulations, you lovebirds. Now let's get something to eat, my treat."

I didn't know why but I suddenly became hungry, so I told them to wait for me to get dressed. The steam from the shower was therapeutic and opened my thoughts as I remembered whose fiancée this was: my homie, my brother, and my friend. I've never had these thoughts or feelings toward any of James's lady friends, so why now?

I didn't understand. I wouldn't ever let a woman come between us, and I shouldn't have even been having that conversation with myself. So I got dressed and called Stacy, a fox that I've been chasing, and told her to meet us at my spot before we left. She's a Dominican and Black beauty; a personal trainer who loves to please big Bobby. I had to pull the trick out of the bag for this one; anything to take my mind off of my friend's girl. Stacy showed up looking sexy as usual, and the competition was on.

"James and Jennifer, this is Stacy."

"Hey, Stacy, nice to meet you; and nice purse. I know a Cole Haan when I see one."

"Kudos; you know your purses, don't you? That's so funny, I'm the same way," Stacy said, and she fit right in. That's what I loved about her. She was sexy, independent, and versatile. She knew her boundaries and how to please a man.

It's funny how everybody's agenda is spawned by reason. There I was, using a lady friend of mine as a pawn to convince myself that I can honestly get over the fact that I was attracted to my best friend's fiancée.

"Why are you looking at me like that, Bobby?" James asked.

"Because you're over there glowing like you're in love, playboy. What's the secret? I might need whatever it is to convince my baby that I'm serious."

"Be careful with what you asking for. You've got to read the fine print before signing the contract," Stacy said sarcastically and Jennifer followed.

"I know that's right, girl. But I think we both have some winners here."

"Well bosses do win, don't we?" James replied. I couldn't stop looking at her, and hung on to her words; recording her voice in my head and remembering such things as how she liked her eggs. Shortly, I came to the reality of the circumstance; this would soon be my sister-in-law. I buried the small feelings I thought I had the minute I realized the truth.

"You know, this is my first time eating here and it's great. I'm going to have to come back soon," I said, and Jennifer responded to my comment.

"Wait . . . wait . . . how are you going to be sitting at a table with two sistahs and brag about restaurant food? James hasn't told you that I can cook?" Jennifer asked.

She was so comical.

"Well don't start bragging and forget to back it up. I'm going to hold you to that."

"I don't think you're ready for Jennifer, man. She got skills, son! James said while paying the bill. We excused ourselves from the table and left the lovebirds alone, and waited outside until they followed.

"Love, to me, is like the end side of the bread. For a while it goes unnoticed, but it's always there when you need it."

"Will you shut up, Bobby; you are so silly," Stacy said bursting in laughter.

"I guess it depends on the person and how much you can trust them. Because the person's perception of love is defined by their personal experiences in the past," Jennifer said.

"And that's what makes it so hard to be yourself when you really want to be. We're so occupied with protecting our feelings from you jerks," Stacy added.

"Hey, hey—I'm not a jerk. I'm an asshole," James interrupted.

We pulled up to the house and I couldn't wait to get out and use the bathroom.

"Hey, we were going to stop by and hangout for a while, but something came up and we have to run. I'll catch you later; and we've got to get together and let our ladies cook."

"Okay, cool. Next weekend maybe; does that sound good? Everyone agreed, and Stacy and I got out of the car and we walked to hers.

"So am I going to see you later or what? And don' tell me yes if something might come up again. You don't like me when I'm sad do you, bootsky?" Stacy asked, poking her lip out with childlike gestures.

"Of course not, baby. But I can't promise anything right now. I'll call you later on, okay?" I closed her car door after she got in and headed in the house.

Settling down at twenty-five was highly unlikely. And besides, with the level that I was on, my pussy rate increased enough to catch Dow Jones's attention to consider me a valuable stock option. The past few weeks were extreme, and this business-shit was like the streets: Shady deals and back stabbing vultures, promoters and their bullshit, and not to mention tenants who ran around in circles explaining everything else except where the money was to pay the rent.

I'm quick to tell someone if you're talking free, you ain't talking to me. It's sad that you have to get ignorant, especially with your own people. I mean, business is business and I covered my end. Maintenance was never an issue and I always maintained a safe environment for the tenants.

I even had a cookout every month free of charge; but when someone tried to bullshit me, I couldn't have that. I had to notify the sheriff's department to put this lady's shit out on the street one day. Yeah, that is embarrassing, but so is being broke. Principal is everything to me and I'm not saying I don't have weaknesses; it's just that my strengths keep my business in perspective.

I woke up early and decided to make use of my time. Checking my mail was a start since I hadn't checked it in a week. So I walked out shirtless with sweats and house slippers to my mailbox, when I noticed a black Crown Victoria with a burly looking male figure in sunshades staring at me. I nodded and got no response. He drove off after lighting a cigarette, so I grabbed my mail and headed back into the house. I remember James telling me about a Lonnie Biggs character, so I called him when I got in.

"Aye, player—I mean, savior."

"Huh?" James replied with a confused tone.

"If you can huh me then you can hear me, man. Get your thumb out of your ass. I was checking my mail when I seen this Ving Rhames looking-ass nigga across the street, and I was the only one getting attention."

James seemed concerned and said, "Did he approach you?"

"Did you hear about a homicide?" I said.

"No."

"I guess not then. Is there something you're not telling me about this guy, because if so, then I need to know—now!"

James became angry. "It's Lonnie, man. He's starting to piss-me-the-fuck-off. Don't worry; I'll take care of it. Jennifer and I are coming over and don't mention any of this to her."

I hung up the phone and proceeded to check my mail. All those missing kid notifications were sickening, and I mean, it's unfortunate and all, but I just wished they'd send me something telling me they found one of them. But I was shocked to see a letter from Xavier "String" Cooper. . . .

Sup, Killa,

It's been crazy since you been out, my nigga. It seems like the days are going slow now that I don't have a homie to bid with, but it's all good. Niggas be talking 'bout ya'll in here and shit, and I'm like, them my niggas! Thanks for the lookout too, holding me down and all. Don't hesitate to ask for anything when I get out, homie. It's like that. Man, I got two years before I leave this place and I can't wait to hit the land.

*I hope you got a job for me because ya boy
gonna need to get on, feel me? Well ya know
I ain't the one to be writing and shit so I'm
gonna get at ya. Be safe out there.*

James and Jennifer wanted to stop by and
chill later that night, and I know I told Stacy I'd
call her, but I decided not to follow up. We've
been hanging pretty tough, and a break from
time to time helps out a lot; or did I just want an
opportunity to glance at Jennifer without the
worry of getting caught?

Being the entertainer that I am, I decided to
purchase a fifth of Hennessey Privilege, Patron
for the left over margarita mix that I had in the
cabinet, along with a variety of music and mov-
ies. They showed up around seven-thirty and I
couldn't have asked for better company.

"Come on in. Did ya'll get everything taken
care of earlier?"

"Yeah, I've been with this nut all day and I'm
ready for a drink—seriously!" Jennifer said rushing into the house.

It was pretty chilly outside and I was ready to
relax. I'm real meticulous about my surroundings
and being in the presence of individuals who add
to your comfort zone, is always a good thing.

"Hey, you're not going to believe where I met
this woman. Okay, you know how bad my road
rage is, right? Well, on my way to a photo shoot
I'm just going crazy trying to get there on time

because I had the key to the building, and you know how photographers are. So I'm honking at this car in front of me and all I see is a head of hair bouncing all over the place with a single finger in the rearview. By now I'm feeling up for a challenge and decide to confront this person, and what I had in mind to tell her couldn't come out, because she was so beautiful," James recounted.

"But believe me I cussed his ass out when I saw an opportunity to speak first." We all laughed and she continued, "I'm serious, it's being a black woman out here, and we have to stand firm. My momma didn't raise no punk now!"

"That's why you have a strong man by your side, too, baby," James said.

After a while I wished I had invited Stacy. I called her and invited her over before making another round of drinks. One conversation I remember having with Jennifer that night was when James went upstairs to the bathroom, and I remember it well, because I thought it was odd that James was using the bathroom upstairs when there was one down here.

Jennifer cut her eyes at me before she spoke. "Can I ask you a question?"

"Sure, what's up," I said.

"Nah, never mind," Jennifer said as she tried to fish for my curiosity.

I responded with, "Speak your mind."

Then she began with, "Truthfully, I think that you are James's other half and that's pretty exciting. I mean, everything that I'm looking for in a man that he's missing, is sitting right here in front of me within arms reach. Do you think I'm wrong for being honest with you?"

I didn't want her to know that I was feeling for her, either, so I said, "I respect your honesty, and my loyalty toward my dog won't allow me to even take your words as a tempting gesture. Honestly, that's why I think we get along so well, and I appreciate the compliment, but I'm not too sure we'd be having this conversation if you weren't under the influence."

She responded with, "Well, Bobby, I definitely didn't want you to take my words the wrong way, but I was merely complimenting your friendship toward my fiancé and identifying the differences between the both of you, and recognizing your good attributes and qualities. I do think that the both of you combined will probably make the perfect man."

She then got up and extended her arm to grab the DVD remote to play the movie. James came back downstairs and we started to watch *Love Jones*. What had just occurred was strange, as if it were a conscience effort on her part to see where my head was, and it tripped me out. Jennifer and I were two consenting adults, and knew that the conversation we'd had were just words with no substance behind them, or was it?

I remember thinking to myself, *she's a confident trickster.* Or was my perception of myself so potent that the thought of wanting a woman that I could not have was beginning to be the antecedent of my own little secret? When I was seven years old I used to see the gangsters and dope boys get money. I knew then that this was my kinda life.

When I killed Millertime I knew it was the sin of all sins, but I loved my sister and wanted her killer to suffer like she did. I had to live with that decision and that was my kinda burden. And in the end we are responsible for decisions we make in our lives, and every move that we make, whether big or small, affects the next step, so I chose to move with extreme caution. And I refuse to let anyone come between me and my happiness. Maybe these feelings were just a phase, or maybe the life I led years back, and who I was before that moment, was just a phase, but Jennifer . . . was my kinda girl!

LONNIE BIGGS
6 years back . . .

I've done a lot of things in my life and I've never considered myself an Angel, but I didn't deserve to lose my only son.

"For as much as it has pleased Almighty God to take out of this world our deceased, Melvin Biggs, and looking for general resurrection in the last day in the life of this world to come through our Lord Jesus Christ, by the sweat of your brow, you will eat your food until you return to the ground. Since from it you were taken; from dust you are and to dust you will return. Let us not mourn a death but celebrate a homecoming. God bless the dead. Amen."

"AMEN."

The preacher continued with the eulogy.

"Melvin Biggs was born on December 17th, 1972, in Atlanta, Georgia, to Lonnie Biggs and Denise Poindexter. He attended three years of high school before he dropped out to pursue a lifestyle to support his personal interest. In the fall of 1992, Melvin had an unexpected blessing when his high school sweetheart gave birth to twins, and he became a proud parent of two healthy boys, whom he loved very much: his first son, Kevin Alexander Biggs, and Keshawn Marquis Biggs.

"Melvin Biggs was loved by many people in so many different ways. He touched the lives of everyone that knew him and was always there for whoever called and needed him. Melvin always spoke his mind and told it like it was, whether you wanted to hear it or not. He had no regrets and made no apologies. He loved the life he lived and lived the life he loved. Melvin suffered a tragic loss last month, June 19th, 2000, when someone endearing to him was taken. He was never the same. Later the Lord called Melvin home to rest on July 23rd, 2000.

"He leaves to cherish his memory, two eight-year-old sons, Kevin Alexander Biggs and Keshawn Marquis Biggs, his father, Lonnie Biggs, his mother, Denise Poindexter, and a host of aunts, uncles, cousins, friends and family."

The pastor closed the procession with a prayer before we departed.

Putting the pieces together wouldn't be difficult at all. My memory was clouded, so I headed to the bar for some holy water. All my life I've been feared, but in the society we live in, you can't take shit from anybody. I established my career on fear, so I guess I've learned over the years to embrace the ability to be careless about anything that doesn't concern me as an individual.

That being said, whoever takes from me will most definitely pay! And the mothafucka who deprived me of what little happiness I acquired, will not walk this earth with any sense of security as long as I have breath in my body. I have my share of enemies, but not too many even knew that I had offspring, so I don't think that his death was in retaliation to get me. But I'll shake some trees to get the information that I need, and utilize my efforts to identify and eliminate the son of a bitch. Some people owe me favors in these streets and it's time to collect. I'm the wrong killer to fuck with, the wrong man to piss off, but the right one to prey on a predator. I'm the LAW.

After a few shots, I went to pay my source a visit. A two-bit loser from the eastside who keeps me updated with information from time to time. I pulled up to him and he got in. We drove to an isolated area, just in case I had to twist an arm. I'm going to get to the bottom of this shit. The whole world is turning into a toilet bowl and if I had the opportunity to flush it, then shit, I would, quicker than a whore could quote her price. All of us are going to hell in the end.

These peasant, pieces-of-shit community leaders milking profits from the poor, and little ungrateful bastards are turning Dr. Martin Luther King's dream into a nightmare. I guess we're all worth more, dead than alive. Well, call me the reaper, vigorously off to collect a head for a debt owed for the death of Melvin. I turned down the radio and looked the kid in his eyes. His reaction was as if he knew my intent. I got straight to the point.

"Tell me about that homicide last week at the motel that made the eleven o'clock news all week."

I showed him a picture. "Do you see a resemblance? He was my son, and I want to know everything that you heard about his murder."

The kid immediately knew what I was talking about, but was acting reluctant to give me what I asked for. "Man, I've been helping you out and shit, but this one has a history, Lonnie. I can't."

I became irate. "No, you are going to tell me everything." I reached over and choked him with his seatbelt while I lit a cigarette and pointed it toward his eye, and that's when the rat squealed.

"Okay, okay. Do you know who your son was in these streets? He was famous! He was the nigga everybody could see themselves as being. We didn't call him anything else other than MILLERTIME."

Now with more information than I had before, my incentive to solve my son's murder tripled. It's not too often that folks in my parts volunteer information, so I took it. There was a prostitute in particular that I'm pretty sure knew what I needed to know. I pulled up to her by the curb and flashed a bill to get her attention. It was getting late.

"Kind of slow around here, isn't it?"

"What do you want, Lonnie? Is that my loot that you owe me for all of the freebees that I gave you?" she asked.

"How many times have I kept you outta jail, and let you work these streets without worry?

Bitch, don't start with me. Get in. I got some questions to ask."

She was really starting to piss me off and I would hate to bust her up in public, so I gave a frustrated look but she kept talking. "Not this time, Lonnie. The last person that entered your car got out a human ashtray. Yeah, baby, bad news travels fast."

And that's when I snapped. "Have you ever sipped soup through a straw, bitch?"

"What?"

"Because you will after I break your cum-guzzling jaw. Now get in the fucking car before I bury you in something hollow!"

She got in and I took her to Memorial Drive Café. I've been frequenting this particular location in attempt to run into someone who owes me an explanation. This was his favorite café, and I just hope to see him in here one of these days. The waitress approached us and uttered, "Hi, Detective, will you be having the regular?"

"Not today, sweetheart. I'm going to try something new."

"What will it be then, hun?"

"Steak—well-done, with a potato; chives and sour cream, and a side of cauliflower and a coke. Oh! I'm sorry, and a glass of water for the lady."

"You could have at least got me a muffin," the whore said.

"Yeah, that would have been thoughtful. I need to know about Millertime and any beefs that he was in that led up to his death."

I guess the thought of losing the control of her jaw assisted her lips to keep moving. She gave me a lot of useful information.

"Millertime was respected for his trade and he didn't have problems, not even with other pimps. It was a shock to hear about his murder, but I can tell you that he did live a double life, and was even talking about leaving the track to pursue other dreams. Somebody had to have changed his perspective, a pastor or something. Whoever it was really influenced him.

"But you know what? He did have the hots for this girl named Pamela Williams. He was head over heals about her. In fact, she was killed about a month and a half before he was killed. Men went crazy over that girl, and I wouldn't be surprised if she was killed over jealousy."

She spilled the beans and told me everything; and I believed her. She'll need me before I ever need her again. I had no more questions to ask.

"So that rules out the suspicion of random actions."

She replied with, "Pretty much, sugar. Whoever killed Millertime wanted him dead for a reason, and your guess is just as good as mine."

I gave the whore my leftovers and tipped the waitress before I headed to my sister's house in Decatur to drop off some money. So far, there were no leads on Millertime's murder until I asked to be put on the case. That name Pamela Williams definitely needed to be looked in to; and I couldn't wait to get to the office and look her up.

"Oh, yeah, I remember that case," another detective said passing by Lonnie Biggs's desk. "She was found murdered in her apartment but her killer was never found. And get this, her brother insisted that we find justice for her and gave me this patriotic speech, only to get busted with a firearm a month or so later, and charged with robbery himself."

I began to look deeper into Pamela's file and found she had a sibling named Bobby Williams, who didn't have the worst record, but he just looked suspicious. I don't think that it's just a coincidence that he was busted the day my son was killed, and I just new that he had something to do with it. The prostitute did mention that my son was seeing his sister, and that he wasn't the type to go stir crazy over women. His business was women and things weren't adding up. There had to be a missing component and I was sure to get to the bottom of this mess.

In my years spent in the criminal enterprise that we call America, I've learned that a watched pot never boils, and that being said, it eliminates the possibility of forgiveness. I hope this Bobby Williams guy enjoys his time in prison, because his life sentence will truly begin after his release!

THE SECRET

"Who the fuck is Jennifer? I know your woman's name is Stacy and you've been with her before me, but who is this other bitch. I won't be disrespected. So what am I, nigga? Number two, three, or four?"

"I'm gonna act like I didn't hear that, sweet daddy, because if Stacy or this Jennifer bitch was handling their business, you wouldn't be spending time with me then, huh?

"Stop exaggerating Coco, you knew what time it was when I met you. You're catching feelings girl and that's not cool."

"Don't anybody fuck you the way that I do! Don't I please you the right way?" Coco asked.

"Yeah," I said.

"Ain't I down for you and keep this deep pussy wet for you?" she continued her line of questioning.

"Yeah."

"Don't you love me and wanna be with me?" she asked.

"Not exactly, and I thought we talked about this already. Stop trying to change me, you're fighting a losing battle, baby. I like what we have and you don't want for anything, so why change? It might get worse if we do," I replied and she didn't take it to kindly.

"Fuck you, nigga, you ain't shit. And if it wasn't for your money, I wouldn't fuck with you so hard anyway." She tried to boss up and I had to let her know who was really running the show.

"Bitch, shut up! You ain't ever seen my money and never will. You ain't shit but imitation crab-meat. You're petty as hell! You might be fine, but somebody is tired of that pussy, and that person is me. You're wasting my time. Maury Povich is on and I ain't trying to end up on there with yo' ass—so step! And don't bother coming by my club anymore. Groupies like you bring the prop-erty value down. I'm a bad influence on the word love, baby. Waiting on me is like trying to ice skate uphill. So do yourself a favor and get a life."

Coco was obviously upset and tried to leave with dignity. "I'm gonna graduate from beauty school, you black bastard, so you can stop it with those whack-ass jokes. And when I walk out, don't ever think about calling me again. I ain't got to put up with this shit, so kiss this."

She gave me the finger and that's when I sent her home with something to grow on.

"Real inspirational, Coco; and I wouldn't be proud showing everybody that IQ score of yours. I am King, bitch!"

I balled up some paper and threw it at her as she turned and headed out. I became angry with myself immediately after my door slammed. Coco had totally changed since I'd first met her, and we went from understanding and pleasing each other all the way, to her trying to break into my phone records using cell phone spyware. Oh no, she had to go!

I sat down, grabbed a left over slice of pizza from the night before, and thought about what had just happened. It's been six months of internal and extremely covert battles with myself. My private crush was difficult to deal with. Jennifer was like a stain that could not be removed. I tried to rehabilitate myself, but I must confess the odds were against my efforts to disclaim my immoral actions and apologetic behaviors. I couldn't get her out of my mind and it was affecting my sex life.

Karma has played a terrible trick and I was reluctant to give in and give glory to my inclinations towards the flesh. Case in point, I refused to play the game of deceit. I owed James more than that and I knew that he would never understand, so for that reason, I chose to eradicate my disposition by exchanging one bad habit for a good one. Everything happens for a reason and maybe God was giving me a sign that I conceived quite well.

My inability to settle down with one woman had manifested to an undeniable need for variety. A feeling of entrapment prohibited me to show interest in a single woman. And I know that I speak for most people of our time, to say the least, but in my opinion, we cheat because we recognize qualities in others that our lovers are missing, therefore triggering our inhibitions not to remain monogamous. I also believed that if given the opportunity to combine our partners, whether male or female, in order to create the ideal mate, relationships would last a lot longer.

It was my opinion that every man should have three women in his life: his wife, his mistress, and a whore, but it was time to get rid of two. I was almost thirty and it was definitely time to stop playing the field, or was I playing myself? I owed it to Stacy to at least to give our relationship a chance; and besides, after a while, trying to preserve that bachelor's lifestyle fades out. So instead of fighting my feelings with resistance, I decided to embrace them with acceptance. I decided to call Stacy because it was time to let her know how I felt about her.

"Baby, let's see each other more often," I suggested.

"And you're saying that to say what, Bobby; are you ready to give up the variety of women throwing themselves at you?" Stacy said and there was a few seconds of silence as I thought about the step that I was trying to take.

"Babe, I can't prevent women from approaching me, but I only want to be with you. I need a woman who can add to my asset column and not become an expense. I have too many of those already. You amaze me in every way and we talk like best friends. Girl, you just don't know. I know what I want and it's you."

"Oh, babe," she said. My words even shocked me, but I meant them.

"I just don't want to be hurt, that's all," I said and we both laughed.

"Boy, you're so silly."

"Well *you're* not going to talk *me* to death. I got a few things to do, but I'm coming over later," I said.

"Okay, and bring my bag that I left at your house."

"Okay cool, later," I said before ending the call. Shortly after I ended my conversation with Stacy, Jennifer called me crying, unable to get herself together.

"Jennifer, calm down. What's wrong?" I asked.

"It's James; he's not himself and hasn't been for about a week now. Something's wrong and I don't know what to do. He doesn't eat, Bobby, and he accuses me of things that are too personal to discuss. We've been arguing and I'm worried. I just need to vent, but please don't mention it to him," she said.

"I feel you. He has his own way of expressing himself. That's James and I wouldn't take it too personal, girl, that nigga loves you. You're his trophy!" I replied.

"You always say the right things, Bobby," Jennifer said.

"Well you are family," I said.

That was definitely not my place. I've never been the one to solve problems and didn't really care what they were going through, to be honest, but out of respect, I talked to her for a while until another phone call interrupted our conversation. I politely excused myself to see who was on the other line, only to find I had more shit to take care of: a dispute that had gotten out of hand at one of our salons and it was trashed pretty badly.

I headed down there to resolve the matter and to file a report, and when I got there I found out that Stacy and that freak bitch, Coco, had gotten into it after Coco had intentionally made a scene in the shop to get Stacy's attention. A small cat-fight turned into a misdemeanor charge when Coco vandalized the beauty salon. She and Stacy were arrested, even though Stacy was not in the wrong.

I sent an associate to bail my baby out of jail while I stuck around to file the report, and made sure the witnesses were given statements to fill out. James also showed up, coked out of his mind. I was surprised to see him in this condition and so were the others; it was bad for business.

Later, I quickly put two and two together, signifying the issues between Jennifer and himself. I didn't know how long he'd been fucking around but he seemed out of control, and he definitely couldn't conceal it. His actions were dictated by his influence and it was not complimentary. I was embarrassed for both of us as he took initiative to handle the situation with the police. It was a sight to see. It's like the officers didn't take notice to James's mumbled words and explanations regarding the salon, as they detected his strange behavior. They concentrated more on his conduct and gestures before questioning his character; therefore, directing their attention toward him.

"Sir, have you been drinking?"

"No, sir, I don't drink and drive . . ." James said.

"Well, sir—" The police officer was interrupted by James's absurd comment.

". . . But I'll drive while I'm drunk, ha, ha."

James was fucked up and the cops knew it.

"Sir, I would appreciate it if you wouldn't interrupt me again. There is no reason to question you, sir. We are convinced that you are under the influence."

He was sweating and wasn't even dressed appropriately enough for any occasion other than laundry day. The police officers detained him for his suspicious behavior and I found out later that upon searching him at the station, the deputies found two grams of cocaine, three dollars in quarters and a childhood photo. He tested positive for cocaine and was charged with possession. I never asked him about the content in his pocket, but always wondered about the change.

His bond was set and he was released as well as Stacy.

Both returned the following month. The judge dismissed Stacy's charges due to numerous statements proving that she was defending herself, and the fact that Coco failed to appear in court also made things easier.

On the flip side of things, James was ordered by the court to admit himself to a rehab facility for a period of six months, giving him a good break. It was involuntary and he had no option but to complete the requirements of the center, and if not, then he had to do mandatory jail time. The only things that James was missing were the tabloids and maybe a segment on Access Hollywood, because he was living an E-True Hollywood Story. Rehab was hard for him but it was definitely for the best.

Jennifer took it hard and grew impatient because of the visitation restrictions. I was in total control of the record label and had to step it up as operational manager. I saw some changes that needed to be made. I put more money into our marketing strategy for Vgo D'artiste to push his sophomore album titled "Rep Yo' City," as well as promoting Sydne Renee to the fullest. Everything is a con if you ask me, but I really believed in these artists so there was no reason to mislead our listeners. What we needed was something that captured the essence of true beauty, a song that set the standard for the talent that's under our corporate umbrella, and Vgo was just the artist to make that happen.

"What's up, Vgo!" I said when he answered.

"What's good, boy! I'm in the studio blessing these tracks; everything straight?"

"Yeah, we good; I just wanted to run something by you and figured I'd call. You know, we need a track that's going to set the standard for our movement. A song that serves as an anthem for women, but from a man's perspective if you know what I'm saying. . . ."

"Yeah, I'm feeling that! What do you have in mind?" he asked before I continued.

"We need a song that will bridge the gap between the battle of the sexes: an answer to all their questions and concerns; and we're going to call it "My Kinda Girl." He began to laugh and I knew he'd seen my vision.

"Man, I'm already thinking about the hook. We gonna kill them with this one."

"Not yet though, let's get the album done first; but that's gonna be the next single for the up-and-coming album. We're going international with that one!" I said with excitement, and we got off the phone soon after.

Building an image for the company was complete and now it was time to take over! We toured for three months, and in between time, I encouraged everybody to record more. Sales increased and profits soared, proving the hustling efforts of the record label as a unit. We ran our company like a democracy and the more we worked, the more we got paid.

At the end of the year, after growing a relationship with our affiliates at Nason Mathias Marketing firm, we were officially being recognized as a major record label. People saw me as the new face for Good Game Records, and even though being the king is what we intend to be, I hated being "that guy." Corporate smiles and jealous admirations were my new surroundings. The atmosphere was like a disease and I tried hard not to get the virus. The industry sucks you in and makes you believe that you can't be touched.

I wasn't too impressed with the fabulous lifestyles that nigga's were willing to sell their souls for. Just give me the money, the hell with the fame. Business was business, and James knew that the label was in good hands, even though his situation was the butt of many after-hour jokes. The new hires and interns would hear them mostly.

"Hey, I heard the owner is in rehab preparing for a movie role!"

"Nah, I heard he was up for three days jump roping in the same position."

"Oh yeah, I heard when he's high he acts like Samuel L Jackson."

A lot of the jokes I've heard were funny, I can't deny that, but the team wins the games and the coaches lose them.

James was dealing with a lot and didn't need to know at that time that a couple of guys, who he called friends, had been stealing money. But he'd take notice to our new policy when he returns to the office and finds out that they were replaced.

Sydne Renee and Vgo D'artiste were on the Top-10 on 106 & Park, and even caught the attention of *Vibe* and *XXL* magazine for an article on separate issues. Even though they were on the same label, we wanted them to have their own image. Phone calls were pouring in with requests for interviews and appearances and I turned down a few, but was proud when I was asked to be on the front cover of *J'adore magazine*, my favorite hip-hop/lifestyle publication.

I had to redirect a couple of questions about James because of how they were directed. My mom used to tell me to never give someone a stick to hit you with, and I chose not to entertain their interest in slandering my boy.

Even though we couldn't hide the fact that the founder of Good Game Records had been in a drug rehabilitation center for six months, while a convict took control during his absence, they still shed light on the more positive issues, and primarily focused on what good we were doing in our community.

I loved the issue, but James didn't.

"I don't like it," James said, tossing the magazine on the counter. At the peak of our company's success he wasn't there, even though he had nothing to worry about.

That's when the jealousy kicked in.

"J'adore is a step-up, and they have a national subscriber list of fifty thousand readers and counting! That's a huge market of readers who will convert to our listeners, you know that. Look, I'm over here doing the best I can and we miss you at the label."

I gave him a poster with the signatures of all of our staff. He snatched it and looked at me before glancing at it.

"I'm ready to get out of here, man, this shit is killing me. But I'm proud of you dog. Remember after the funeral when we planned this shit?" James asked.

"I know what you're going through, dog. At least you got six months for your troubles—I got six years! So just shut up, do the rest of this small time and come back to the spotlight."

He knew my intentions were not a threat toward his position, and he understood my decisions were beneficial for the company, but his isolation was affecting his morale. It was for that reason that I included Jennifer in all of our business affairs, so he would be fully aware of every move that was being made. When it comes to money, trust is an inconvenient reward, so to eliminate conflict between James and me, Jennifer was carefully informed. And besides, who else but the one you love, would you address to spy on your best friend?

It was already five months into James's court ordered stay, and I was already planning a release party for his return. After the article, the only thing I was turning down was my collar. I learned how to pimp the system and use my industry connects to plug our company projects. People liked my character, and even though I wasn't an artist, radio personalities often asked me to stop by the station to represent.

Stacy and I were on our way to New York for a couple days to get away. *Color Purple* was our favorite movie and she was excited to see the play on Broadway. Our flight was at eleven-thirty at night and we agreed to meet at the airport because she had a prior engagement. I left the radio station at 7 PM, but I still had to stop by the house to pick up a few things. Jennifer called me when I jumped in my ride.

"Hello?"

"Hey, are you still leaving tonight?"

I noticed my phone battery was extremely low and was about to die. "Yeah, I'm on my way to the house now to feed the dogs and then I'm out."

"Okay, well, have fun, and tell Stacy I said don't spend all of your money."

"Well you know how you women are—always a trick up your sleeve."

"Hmm, is that right? She asked.

"I'll tell her that you said what's up."

"Okay, bye."

My low battery signal flashed so I called Stacy.

"Hey, baby!" she said with excitement.

"Hey, you know the airport is going to be busy and I know how punctual you are, but you have to be checking in by ten."

"I'm right down the street from the airport at Dawn's house, so I'm gonna need you to follow your own advice, baby. I'm so excited, so don't miss the flight!" she said.

"I'm headed to the house now to freshen up. I can't wait to see you. I love you, Sophia."

Stacy laughed before responding, "I love you, too, Harpo; bye."

I stopped at the light and took a deep breath before I realized that I really meant it when I told Stacy that I loved her. I smiled almost immediately. I cracked my window to toss my cigarette when I heard some white boys listening and bobbing their heads to our new single, and I remember thinking to myself, *life couldn't get better than this.*

It was already eight-forty when I got home and I was ahead of my schedule. My house was pitch-black as I searched for the light switch so I could find the stairs. The only thing on my mind at that point was getting ready. Stacy was very punctual and I hated to hear her mouth about wasting time, so I ran upstairs and turned on the shower in the hallway. I took a leak before I figured it would be better to wash up in my room. I turned the water off, only to hear an identical sound in my room down the hall.

I did six years in prison and would be damned if I let the sound of water frighten me, so I flushed the toilet and headed to my room. The closer I walked toward my room, the more clearly I heard the trickled sound as it enhanced my curiosity. I opened the door only to be in darkness again, and was lured to my private bathroom by the dimmed light, surrounded by steam. I was enticed by the activities of who kept it occupied.

Stacy knew that we had to be at the airport and how I couldn't sleep on flights, so I guess she figured she would volunteer to extract what energy that I had left. DAMN, I LOVE HER! I started taking my shoes off and undressing; I always have time for a quickie!

Standing by the door, I got excited just looking at my woman's figure, it was almost blurred by the showers glass sliding doors. It was hard to see but I could imagine Stacy's moist body, riding my soul pole with satisfying measures. I grabbed my penis and with it in hand, then grabbed the shower handle to slide it open for a surprised entry.

"I hope you don't mind me using the spare key, Bobby?"

"Jennifer?" Suddenly my heart lost its mind as I allowed a similar déjà vu to play out with no hesitation.

I gave in.

"What are you doing here"? I asked.

She directed the showerhead in a downward position to give me every moment of her attention, as she purposely fondled her natural breast, pinching those dark brown, half of dollar round nipples. A million questions ran through my mind: like how long has she planned this, and how good is her pussy?

By the time I left, I figured I would have known the answer to at least one. Jennifer looked at me with a body so perfect, she made the water drool. Moreover, she said with an arrogant voice, "I like your shower better than mine, wanna know why?"

"Why?" I replied.

"Because it's room for two; now get in, both of you!" she chuckled.

I guess my dick was so hard, you would think it deserved its own social security number. I got in the shower and she grabbed my member, pulling me close enough to whisper in my ear, "Checkmate."

She put her tongue in my ear as we let over eight months of anticipation out and into the open. Her heavy breathing and conventional moans turned me on like no other. She turned around and gave me a show, shaking her apple ass before putting me inside of her. I grabbed her hair as she demanded that I go deep and hard. I tried to think about my girl but I couldn't remember her name— fuck it, it ain't a crime if you don't get caught!

The sound of water running and skin smacking fueled my stamina. The feeling of our physical connection satisfied my search for my kinda girl. Her hot, moist and humid love trap took to my penis like an infant who anxiously accepts a pacifier. Her pussy fit my dick better than my own hand.

The steam was getting me light headed, so we relocated to the bedroom. She jumped on the bed like a schoolgirl with week's worth of gossip. I've been with a lot of women and I know enough to say that a condom would only subtract the true sensation of such a beautiful experience.

There she was, nude on my bed with her secret garden trimmed just the way I liked it, and eager to taste me. She crawled to the edge of the bed and sprayed a little of my cologne in the air, before laying on her stomach and inserting me into her mouth.

"I'm addicted to your scent, Bobby. It puts me in a trance and all I can think about is swallowing your dick until it stretches my throat. It makes me want to be your experimental queen bitch!" she said while jerking me with her right hand. She was enjoying her test drive with intentions to pursue a quest for the top performance in case she decided to engage again, in the near future.

She gagged, choked, spit and licked on my dick as my brown marbles rolled like snake eyes in a crap game. Jennifer looked up at me as I interrupted her program. I got on top of her and kissed every inch of her body until I buried my face in her precious little secret. Why a secret you ask? Because if her pussy was mine, I wouldn't tell anybody how good it was. I was eating that sweet stuff like I had sugar diabetes.

Her body jerked and she told me to stop.

"Get on top of me, daddy. I want you to put this pussy on the injured list until you come back from New York to fix it." No bitch has ever talked to me or had me gone like this, including Stacy. I participated in her role-play.

"Say pretty please."

"Pretty please, Bobby."

"I want you to receive this dick. I want you to feel this dick."

"I want to feel it in my stomach, baby."

I grabbed my dick while I looked at her biting her lip; her eyes closed while she ran her fingers through her hair. This was the sexiest bitch alive to me, and stroking Jennifer was the greatest feeling to me besides checking a fat bankroll. Electricity was in the air and it seemed like the roof was going to collapse and the bed was going to break. We gave a completely new meaning to the word fucking. She bit my ear like Holyfield before telling me that her pussy was about to explode with laughter. When her orgasm came, she grabbed me tight and moved with a motion so gratifying; I too, was on my way. My head became hot and was ready to add more mess to the sheets.

I pulled out and Jennifer jumped up immediately as if she took notice to a problem.

I guess the only problem to her was seeing good sperm go to waste. She grabbed my dick and jerked it in her mouth, with arousing groans and playful tongue action. I felt it about to erupt and took a handful of her hair as I watched and heard her deep throat me until I let go. I lay down speechless, but with a whole lot to say.

"Damn, baby, you're the truth."

She looked me in the eyes, passed me a cigarette, and lit it while she spoke, "You don't come across as being exactly a chump in the sheets yourself. Baby, my thunder pussy hasn't roared like that in quite some time now. What's your secret, calcium?" We both laughed but I knew the position that we both were in, so I decided to break the ice.

"But seriously, Jennifer . . ." She cut me off before I could finish.

"Shhh—I know the circumstances and I do love James, and I admit I did feel guilty when I used to think about you, and it was wrong, but I just can't explain it and I can't explain where we go from here.

"It's something about you, Bobby, and I can't comprehend, myself. Let's just go where the day takes us and keep this secret between us, because I think we both know that what we could have won't go as far as the bedroom." She placed her lips on mine. "Okay, baby?"

I let out a sigh of relief just knowing that she has been contending the same temptation that haunted me, and it helped me understand her anonymous visit. I kissed her back. "Okay." And like that, we were back to ourselves again.

Stacy was back on my mind and Jennifer was just, Jennifer. It's like we blacked out in order to allow our fantasies to live for a moment before we went on to proceed with our regular lives. We even took separate showers before getting dressed and parting ways. It was already ten o'clock, so I called Stacy from a pay phone. She was already at the airport checking in her bags. I only had a carry-on so I didn't worry too much about being there too early, because even though I might be a little late, I'm always still on time!

The smell of sweet sex covered the air in my room when I left, and the last thing I needed on my mind when I saw Stacy was regret.

I caught a cab to the airport; the very same airport that I ran my first con. I got there at ten-thirty, and I was in desperate need of a drink. Stacy met me at a bar in the airport and when she saw me, she gave me a penitentiary hug, as if she hadn't seen me in some years. I remember thinking, damn; my fucking ear is killing me! I hoped Jennifer didn't leave me with any bruises.

After we boarded the plane, I was already getting tired. Stacy handed me a hip-hop magazine that she bought me and I declined. "Baby, I know you get restless on flights, so I bought you something to read, are you all right?"

"Yeah, I'm fine. It's just been a busy day and it's catching up with me"

Stacy kissed me on the cheek. "I love you, Bobby."

"I love you too, baby."

As soon as I closed my eyes I thought about my mother's battle with cancer and Pamela's battle before her death. A moment of weakness can ultimately alter your life; and we're forced to live with our decisions in the end and battle our own demons until we're forgiven. I'm in too deep now. I've crossed the line. My best friend's fiancée has become my secret lover and this is a battle that I knew that I couldn't win.

The plane took off and I began reliving my day while listening to Sydne Renee's smash hit "Lova Friend." It definitely put a smile on my face because the life that I was living was amazing. Here I was on a plane to New York listening to a song that I genuinely love and would purchase, and this artist is actually signed to my label! This is truly everything that I wanted in life, and there's nothing that I wouldn't do to protect it. After taking a deep breath I kissed Stacy, and I was ready until I thought about my dogs. I'D FORGOTTEN TO FEED THEM!

THE ARRIVAL

"Hi, this is your captain speaking on behalf of the flight crew. We would like to thank you for choosing U.S. Airways Express, operated by U.S. Wisconsin. Please remain seated as we are pulling up to the terminal. The weather conditions are fair at a relaxed seventy degrees, and don't forget to set your watch, ladies and gentlemen; we are now in Eastern Time.

"It's now four-thirty in the morning. Please be careful when opening the overhead compartments, the luggage tends to shift during the in-air flight. Once again, we would like to thank you for choosing U.S. Airways and we are looking forward to seeing you on future flights."

"We're here, baby." Stacy's energy put a smile on my face. I turned my phone on when we got to the room and I had some messages. I hadn't checked them since my phone died in Atlanta.

"You have three new messages; to play your messages, press one. New message, received at 7:20 PM."

"Hey, man, this is James; you and Stacy have fun, hit me up when you get back; peace."

"New message, received at 7:25 PM."

"Hello, Mr. Williams, it's Taneish with J'Dore Magazine. Sorry I wasn't there for the shoot but I heard your interview, and thanks for the shout out. I'm glad you liked the article, and we've got to

do some charity work together. Talk to you soon. Bye."

"New message, received at 7:31 PM."

"Bobby, that is the last time . . ."

I erased that message before I could spell it. Coco was so thirsty and I tried to ignore her, hoping she'd just fall off my bumper.

"New message, received at 8:30 PM."

"Bobby, this is Jennifer. I'm a little aggravated and I just don't want to deal with James right now. If you talk to him, tell him how much I love him. I'm at home and will see him tomorrow. Have a safe trip. Bye."

"You have no more messages. Good-bye."

The message from Jennifer was at eight-thirty, before I even got to my house and she was already there, so why would she leave that message? The only reason that I could think of was to set-up an alibi.

She'd planned that night well with no mess to cleanup. It's only been a couple of hours and I was already expecting a serious consequence for this one. The trip was just what we needed. I loved screenplays, and I had just as much fun as I did when I was with my family years back.

Along with some shopping, fancy restaurants, and expensive nightlife hangouts, we had a hell of a trip. New York is the shit, but I don't think that I could move there. Three days was enough. We returned during the morning time, and was hungry as shit, so we caught a cab to the nearest

Waffle House. Stacy looked concerned and worried.

"What's wrong, baby?"

We sat at a booth and she put her hand on my cheek, hesitating shortly before speaking, "When we first met, I was uninformed and empty. I filled myself with self-reliance and it conditioned my ability to adapt to loneliness, but you overwhelmed me with love and guided me mentally, physically and spiritually. I'm yours and I offer everything to you, Bobby. I love you and I want to have your baby."

Hearing news like that was already filling enough, combined with the joy that I felt, I no longer had an appetite. I didn't want to jump to conclusions, so I asked, "Are you pregnant?"

"Yes."

I was happy, and sitting across from her at that point, was too far, so I got up, sat beside her and placed my lips on hers, sealing our decision, together as parents. My life was finally seeing the light at the end of the tunnel. God's divine plan for me was unraveling and I humbly accepted.

After we ate, we had Stacy's mother pick us up. A part of me said that I was rushing into things with Stacy, to convince myself that my feelings for Jennifer were just a phase. I couldn't help but compare the two; and I'm ashamed to say who always turned out to be the victor.

I guess the fact of the matter was that Stacy was my fourth and goal, and Jennifer was my touchdown. Over the years, in these streets and in prison, I've learned to play on emotions for personal gain, and to manipulate plenty of situations to fill my plate. I accepted the reality of con, because by now, I was my own victim.

I couldn't continue to lie to myself, but I didn't want to lose Stacy. I loved her sincerely but I craved to be involved with Jennifer. I looked at Stacy and all I could think of, was her idea of me being the perfect man for her. Was I wrong for not intervening with her happiness; or should I be blamed for keeping a pretty bird imprisoned in a cage of sugarcoated love, out of my own selfish impulses?

Stacy had to run some errands with her mother, and since her car was in the shop, I let them use mine. So I had them drop me off at the house only to find out that it had been broken into. Whoever the intruder was, they knew what they were doing and wasn't there for anything material. Nothing that I initially expected to be taken was missing, and the only thing that was tampered with, were my files and court documents. Paper was everywhere and Stacy was annoying me with her fucking rhetorical questions.

"Do you want me to stay?"

She knew that she didn't want to and so did I, so I gave her the look and started to straighten up. The police would have only pissed me off so it was useless to call them; me, a convict who turned his life around, only to succeed and live the life that they admired. That was harassment just waiting to happen.

The longer I thought about it, the more I put it together. Someone who breaks into a house to read is quite strange to the average victim, but not if that victim has something to hide. In my case, I didn't, but the perpetrator obviously believed so.

In addition, the neighborhood that I lived in wasn't exactly a target area for a typical break-in. This person has probably been watching me, this person was looking for information, this person could only be LONNIE BIGGS.

I didn't really feel threatened because if he wanted me dead, I probably would have been already. Therefore, I neglected to mention it to James, assuming that the truth eventually would come to the light. I'd have to admit that this guy was dirt under my nails and I wouldn't mourn, not once, if I heard that a groundhog was his new mailman. My thoughts were interrupted by my "Love and Happiness" ring tone; it was Stacy.

"Hey, sweetness," I said.

"Bobby, I'm at the police station waiting on a tow truck to pick us up and bring us back home."

"What the fuck, Stacy! Why are you at the station?"

"My mom and I were on our way to Pier 1 Imports when a scary looking man drove up alongside of us, baby. And then he followed us until I drove to the police station, and then he disappeared. I was scared, Bobby, he didn't look friendly at all.

"We went into the station to notify an officer about the incident and they took my information, but that was about it. When we walked back outside, baby, the car was fucked up. Tires flat, windows busted with a dent in the front hood; what's going on, Bobby? Do you know this nigga who was following us?"

It took some time for me to respond and I threw a lamp to release some tension. I took a deep breath and then spoke, "I think I have an idea and don't worry, it's nothing to stress over. What kind of car was he driving?"

"A black Crown Victoria," she said.

"Okay, wait for the truck then come home. I'll get you a rental; bye." I hung up the phone and threw it on the couch. Lonnie was fucking with the wrong one, and his ticket has just expired. Problems were nothing to me, so I didn't let this situation bother me at all. But the difference between this issue and the ones before was that I knew their reasons. I guess the only way to find out was to ask, because Bobby Williams didn't run from anybody. The thought of Stacy going through such an experience sent chills down my spine, and shit was getting a little too close to home—literally.

I was eager to see her and when she arrived. I promised her as long as she was with me, she would always be safe. It seemed like as the days advanced, I grew closer and closer to Stacy; the old me would have been more concerned about the car and not the passengers. We took a cab to Avis to rent a car and it gave me some time to make an appointment to have an alarm system installed; and to make plans for James's welcome home party.

It was only ten days before his release and I didn't have shit organized for him. I did know that he loved Sydne Renee's new single and we could kill two birds with one stone to promote her album, so we were good on entertainment for the night. Along with two first-class tickets to the Cayman Islands for a week, I think he'll enjoy himself pretty well. Planning everything wasn't hard and I was glad I finally got it out of the way. That's when he called.

"Hey, dog! Did you talk to Jennifer the night that you and Stacy left for New York?"

"Nah, but she left me a message saying that she wasn't feeling too well and that you two got into an argument. She told me to tell you, but it slipped my mind; my bad, why?"

"Because we had an argument and now she's trying to occupy her time with more work to avoid being around me so much, like we used to be. I don't understand. I told her that she didn't have to work at all, and she told me that she needed to, in order to preserve our relationship. We've been hand in hand all this time, and now she talking about small distances and shit. Can you believe that?"

I knew where else her time was going and I didn't want to interfere at all, so I took Jennifer's side. "Yeah, that's right, man; Stacy and I are real close because we don't be up and under each other all the time. You love her, don't you?"

"You already know," he replied as if I were asking a stupid question.

"And she loves you, right?"

"She can't live without me; we're a perfect match."

The only thing about stabbing your friends in the back is hearing their concerns and looking in their eyes when they're hurt, knowing that you're the cause of all their pain. It would have been much easier to deal with if I didn't know him, because even if I stabbed a stranger in the back, I could at least watch him walk away afterwards. I continued to play my part.

"Then you got to respect her privacy. At least she had the decency to call me and let me know what the deal was, ya know?"

"Yeah, you're right, homie, about most of what you're saying!"

"What do you mean?"

"Well she called you twice that night; once at seven-fifteen and another at eight-thirty."

"Huh?" I said surprisingly.

"I get the bill every month, my friend."

"Oh yeah! You know what; she did wish me a good trip. I remember now because I was kind of rushing her off the phone to hurry and click back over to speak to Stacy. Damn! I know you been away, but don't go hallucinating on me. Are you okay?"

"Yeah, I guess I have been here too long."

We continued to talk a little more and I told him about the car situation but didn't get into too much detail about it. When I hung up, Stacy was signaling me to get up; she'd signed the papers for the car rental and it was time to leave. I followed behind them and I felt tired, not physically but mentally, and instead of fatigue catching up with me, I felt the truth catching up; and I was only ahead by inches.

I've done a lot of dirt, but this mud was too close to home. Reality was slowly settling in regarding my love triangle, and I emphasize the word *triangle* with confidence because, even though it happened once and it wasn't too late to bury my infliction in the shallowest of graves, I had every intention in the world to continue my faithlessness agenda. But I am selfish and without restraint, I am reckless, I AM A MAN.

If James confronted me, I wouldn't have even insulted his intelligence with excuses and fake smiles, or try to play sides and put the blame on Jennifer. Those are weak actions for a weak-ass nigga, and as contradicting as that sounds, there is a difference between that type and me, and anybody who searches for scapegoats to elude their mistakes when confronted, are weak individuals.

I was fully aware that I was wrong and would never think that James would be overreacting if he chose not to associate himself with me anymore. However, I admit that I was weak; not weak minded, but weak for the flesh; the flesh of beauty that was defined by a name, more valuable than a memory. Her name alone will always be involved in my thoughts, and her name was Jennifer.

After we dropped off Stacy's mother, we rushed to the house to make love. Both of us were tired but desperately needed to release some tension that reminded me of a one-way non-stop flight to Pleasureville. We both anxiously waited to get where we wanted to be, dealing with the process as we descended to the proper positions that secured our comfort after frequent experiences of turbulence, before we landed safely.

No words were spoken from our mouths; our bodies did all of the talking. I couldn't help but rub Stacy's stomach in anticipation to hold, hear and look at our creation. I truly felt blessed but cursed at the same time; blessed because my life turned for the best. I was financially stable with a woman who loved me and held my child, along with a career and lifestyle that most dream of, or even are willing to kill for, and my only curse was a deep secret. We all have them, but I couldn't live comfortably with mine; and I would love to meet a man who could.

Jennifer called me later that day with the rest of the details about the party for James, and everything was perfectly prepared just the way I wanted it. Since that portion of my weekly agenda was taken care of, I could focus more of my time on Lonnie Biggs. I found out where he enjoyed most of his meals during the week: a café on Memorial Drive.

I decided to confront the source instead of playing fucking games. I waited and waited until it closed, and he was a no-show. The same shit occurred on the next day as well. Like a game of hide and seek, I was it, but in this case, the stakes were high and I was playing for keeps. I couldn't stick around all day and decided to have one of my soldiers watch for his car between twelve and two in the afternoon, everyday, until he came.

James's release time was at nine o'clock on Monday. It was ironic that around that time last year, I was the one being released from an institution. I had jokes for him just as he had them for me.

"What up, my nigga, do you need to go to the clinic?" I said jokingly.

"Yeah, yeah, real funny, man; I'm starving."

"What's up, baby?" He ran to Jennifer.

She smiled and gave him a hug, followed by a kiss before she spoke, "I don't ever want to fight again. I missed you with an urgent need to re-unite. I was lonely without you. Please don't leave me again. I love you very much."

James placed his forehead on hers and said, "Without you, my heart wouldn't have rhythm and my blood would flow like the rapids. I am all to pieces and you're my adhesive. I love you more than I love myself."

"Get a fucking room, you lovebirds," I said as they started to kiss. I began to feel awkward, so I grabbed Stacy and joined in on the public affection.

We went to eat breakfast and we talked and laughed until our food arrived. There was only one question on my mind that reminded me about the situation with James when he was in rehab, and since he was in my face, I asked him, "Man, why the fuck did you have three dollars in quarters in your pocket the day you were busted?" Everybody reacted as if they were going to ask the same question before laughing.

"Bobby, I was trippin' that whole week, but that day, Jennifer told me that I needed some change in my life and I was so fucked up, that's how I perceived it—literally—so I took the loose cash in my pocket, which was forty-three dollars, and exchanged it at the bank for quarters.

"I was spending change like a nigga robbed a pay phone or some shit! I'm embarrassed to even be talking about this, but the shit is funny, now that I think back."

Jennifer fed him some food as she tried to cheer him up. "Well, baby, that was just a phase and we all go through them."

As I listened to her discussion on temporary phases, I couldn't help but assume that I was involved in most of her remarks as an inside joke or something. Breakfast was slamming and we parted ways afterwards. I wanted James to believe that the day was just as normal as any other was. Since I was a Morris Day fan myself, I picked them up, escorted them to their rooms, and entertained them until it was time to perform later that night at the club.

Jennifer called and told me that James was somewhat disappointed in me because of how much he did when I was released. I had everything set-up perfectly, and it all started when we met up later to—what James was led to believe— eat dinner. When I gave him and Jennifer their two first-class tickets to the Cayman Islands, he was excited.

"Damn; thanks, homie, I needed this. I thought we were going to eat. Why are we pulling up to the club?"

The club parking lot was packed and to keep his surprise a secret, I told him that a local promoter paid for the night and I had to pick up the rest of the deposit before we left. I even urged him to come with me to meet him.

When we walked in the spotlight hit James and it was on! He had to have felt the same way as I did when I'd walked into my surprise party when I got out.

"Welcome back, James!" Vgo yelled before patting him on the back. Everybody else around him followed with their own welcoming gestures and he gave me the strangest look that I have ever seen. A look that said, "I don't deserve this love from you." It's like he wanted to reject my appreciation for what he did for me. My kindness amazed him but he was grateful. This was my brother.

Before the performance, Sydne Renee gave a toast and it was beautiful. It was his night and I loved being apart of his happiness until I got a text that read: MEET ME IN THE STORAGE ROOM- JENNIFER

His night quickly turned into mine as I've anticipated that moment since I left for New York. My actions were comparable to a caged animal unleashed and given back to its habitat. I paced as my skin tingled all over until my hand finally touched the storage closet doorknob. I paused for a moment to reflect on the situation at hand, looking down in contemplation as if I noticed a hundred-dollar bill on the ground. This was exciting and I was driven by passion, but obviously, the cost of it was extremely high and I was all in.

The cracked door shed light on Jennifer when I entered. It was ten minutes until James's birthday announcement, and I only needed five. I embraced her like a coat in the winter and her body reminded me of lying on warm laundry. Jennifer put her head on my chest and begged for a wish that only I could grant.

"I need you to fuck me, Bobby, and don't stop until my anxious wet sugar pussy erupts on your addictive super sweet dick. Stroke me with anger, baby, and make me hate you, daddy. Okay?"

Words to me at that point were a waste of time because it was limited. Jennifer was wearing a black and gray silk Chloé mini dress with matching pumps, and it looked like it was designed to fit her mind-blowing frame.

Four minutes and forty seconds.

Our lips clanged together as our animal instincts took over. I couldn't fit anymore of her ass in my palms, and during our stimulating experience, there was only one thing missing: her panties. She took my hand and put it under her dress, placing it on her plump vagina; the size of a baby squirrel's head. I planted my two fingers carefully into her enough not to puncture her clit with my fingernails, maneuvering my wrist and controlling the movement like an aviator pilot, before withdrawing my fingers and placing them in her mouth.

Jennifer kissed me everywhere above my neck while unbuckling my belt. We moved close to the corner together, with eyes in tact and bodies in sync.

Four minutes.

My pants fell and the sound of my Gucci belt buckle hitting the floor was like the starter pistol at the Olympics. I picked Jennifer up and placed her on a case of Jack Daniels. Her breasts bounced and vibrated to the DJ's club mix, as she wrapped her legs and arms around me while moving her body like a snake; she wanted me bad—as if this dick gave her energy to continue living.

Two minutes.

I pulled her dress up and Jennifer became thrilled, awaiting my ingression. She took to my penis like a dope fiend injecting a fix. My hands gripped her soft ass as I went deeper and deeper into her body, watching my dick disappear, and then reappear, again . . . and again; I was a couple strokes in before someone tried to enter the room.

"Hurry up and get that; look at us!" We quickly straightened ourselves and Jennifer hid before I took the chair from the door. It was the bar-back coming to refill the bar.

"Bobby? James asked you to get a case of Hennessy, too?" he asked.

"Yeah, you know how he is, always telling people to do the same shit. I got it, don't worry." He left and it bought us time to get away unnoticed. This was too much for me to go through, but she was too hard to let go. I was into her, and the only way I would ever let go now is if she forced me to.

"Hey, I'm going to walk out and take this case to the bar. Damn, I'm horny. I feel like Tom Cruise. This is some Mission Impossible-type shit here!" We both laughed before leaving.

After dropping off the box, I was and on my way to the VIP to sit with everybody, when the performance was interrupted by an announcement. Then I was called and redirected to the stage to say a few things about James.

When I got on stage I noticed Jennifer, Stacy, and James together in the VIP cheering me on. I threw back the rest of my champagne in a failed attempt to take my mind off the incident that had just taken place, and there I was with a microphone in my hand, Jennifer's sweet smell on my body, and a feeling that I've never had before: an accomplished feeling that I couldn't afford to expose. Situations would be a little less unnerving if Jennifer was the fiancée of some stranger, but the fact that my kinda girl was James's lover, could only be the devil's prank. I was swinging a slow bat at a fast pitch and began to feel the heat a little.

"Excuse me, ladies and gentlemen. Of course, we are all here to welcome James home, and couldn't be more thankful for the sweet melody of Sydne Renee—that girl is something! And I'd like to thank everyone here who attended, and being here with us tonight to celebrate. James has had my back since I met him seven years ago, and if you know him well, then I'm sure I don't have to explain how much of a friend he is, and how much it means to him that we are all here to-night."

I raised my glass and everybody followed.

"It's because of you James, that my life now is fulfilled. You have assisted, with sacrificial measures, to help me live my kinda life. I want to thank you for everything, and your blessings will come tenfold. We love you, man!"

I handed the microphone back to Morris Day and went back to my table. I think Jennifer felt responsible for my disposition and had expectations to allow our fling to fade away like a hangover in the morning, but the fire between us only proved that our passion was still heavily intoxicated. Stacy approached me with a kiss when I entered the VIP, and James was heartfelt by my speech.

"I didn't know you were so well-spoken, Bobby. You almost sound like a gentleman," James said and Stacy followed while fixing my collar.

"He is a gentleman."

I put my arms around her.

"This is to you, James. This is for the little time in life that we lose in preparation for the big parade we call success."

We partied like rock stars that night, but there was something about it that triggered my perception of reality; a reality which I chose to ignore as long as I was on top of my game. I was satisfied with my cake, but I needed James's too. I was going for a long ride with no rearview mirror, a bad engine, and no idea where I would ultimately end up.

My mom was right when she talked about the choices that we make in life. And I don't think that I had the ability to control mine, if it involved Jennifer. James and Jennifer's flight was the next day at twelve-thirty in the afternoon.

I had Stacy drop them off at the airport and she called me on her way back to see if I wanted a bite to eat, and that's when an associate of mine called to tell me some good news about an individual that I loved to hate. I wasn't expecting any drama so I threw my Braves fitted on, and left the house. I called Stacy to cancel my order because I didn't want to spoil my appetite for my uninvited lunch with LONNIE BIGGS!

LONNIE BIGGS:
Information Gathered

It's been six years of patience and the time has come. I know everything that I need to know and will use what little information I have accumulated over the years, to get the rest of the story. Monitoring Bobby Williams while incarcerated helped me find out who was closest to him, and planting the seed of fear began with his friend James Fullerton, a nickel and dime, petty hustler with a dream, who turned CEO on my expense.

We had a good thing going; him being the distributor and I, the supplier in all. But the bastard got hip to my plans for him and pulled out just in time, and turned legit. I guess he was smarter than he looked. But just as I built him up, I will break him down; and Bobby Williams is the key that will give me access to their destruction.

A month or two after his release, I figured I'd pay him a visit to his residence and finally, Bobby Williams and I had seen each other eye-to-eye; just thinking about the only thing that connected us, made me want to empty my clip in him. We stared at each other as I drove away. He stood there in deep thought probably wondering what the fuck just happened. I'm Lonnie Biggs! Which makes him a marked man, and his fate has been sealed with a kiss of death.

136

Every time I look into my grandchildren's eyes, it reminds me of their father's absence, and even though we weren't the closest, it fuels my anger and increases my rage just knowing that I can never apologize to him for all the wrong that I've done in the past. My plan has unraveled and soon, Bobby and James will be eating out the palm of my hand.

I started by breaking into Bobby's house to find illegitimate paperwork to connect them with any illegal activity, in hopes to find something incriminating to deflate their success bubble, but the residence was clean. Shortly after the break-in, I was on my way to the precinct when I noticed Bobby's car, and I drove beside it only to realize that it was one of his whores, and I decided to frighten her.

She was headed in my direction and I tailed her close enough to tap the bumper, and continued to taunt her until she turned the corner and parked in front of the precinct. I kept straight to the garage and parked my car, and when I got to my desk I opened my window to get some air and saw a woman practically demolishing Bobby's car. I guess I wasn't the only person that has a grudge against him. I stood there with a grin as I cheered that petite, sexy bitch on as she bashed his car with no obvious regrets.

Shortly after the girl left, Bobby's girl walked out amazed and upset to see what had taken place. She then left in a tow truck, and it was entertaining to me just knowing that Bobby's day wasn't the greatest. After I turned in some paperwork to cover my tracks for a robbery that I was involved in, I decided to go to the café for a club sandwich and some coffee, but wound up stopping at the house first to put some cash and heroin in the safe.

When I entered my garage, I instantly became agitated when I couldn't help but look at my son's belongings. That shit crowded too much space and I'd even thought about getting rid of it. Honestly, I figured it would be noble of me to keep his property, but all of those boxes were just in the fucking way.

In the midst of separating trash from treasure, I found the missing link to all of the answers to my questions, and my new discovery opened my heart to the significance of revenge; the type of revenge that prepares itself for the perfect opportunity. Not only am I going to eat, but I am also going to celebrate.

The afternoon was cool and today's sunrise had a mild opacity, transparent to a dreadful karma in the likeness of Gabrielle; the angel of death. For some reason I became somewhat relaxed and not so tense when I entered the café. I ordered some coffee and a sandwich while I checked last night's numbers, just to be disappointed once again, but found myself regaining my composure when I flipped to the sports page, until I was interrupted.

"Room for two?"

My eyes were buried in the headline of the newspaper when my attention was distracted. I didn't acknowledge him as I spoke, "I don't have any spare change, so get the fuck . . ."

I looked up and noticed Bobby Williams. "What the fuck are you doing here?"

He wasn't shocked that I was aware of who he was. It was inevitable for us to meet before our showdown. He placed both of his hands on the table and looked down upon me. The server picked up the phone, but I signaled her to hang it up.

"I'm pretty sure you already know. I mean, you have been following me."

"Let's get something straight, killa, whatever it is that you want from me, I don't have it. And looking over my shoulder for some shit that I have no clue of makes me nervous; and you don't want me to be nervous. If you want a war, let me know right now!"

I looked in his eyes for the second time; the same eyes that inherited my son's soul with his insignificant beliefs and fucked up perceptions. What I have planned for him is beyond cynical and for that reason, I won't cheat myself and do him the favor by taking him out back, and cutting his fucking throat.

"You've got balls, kid; coming into my fucking café with your fitted cap and pinky rings, thinking you can intimidate me like some degenerate prick who doesn't know his asshole from his eardrum. As far as I'm concerned, Bobby, you're just a pawn used in a game far beyond your comprehension. You should be more mindful of who you trust and pay more attention to your past. I don't give a fuck about you or your past for that matter, but the expression on your face when this is all over, is a high expectation of mine."

I folded my paper as Bobby stood above me with a confused look that couldn't correct itself, as if he didn't expect the response that I gave him. He stared at me with a posture insinuating that I should continue with my lesson, but I had no more words for him, only incentives. I removed my frames before speaking to give him a reason to leave.

"So ask yourself something, young blood; are you here to ask the questions or are you here fishing for answers?" I placed my Beretta on the table. "Now get the fuck out of here, you're ruining my appetite."

Bobby fixed his hat and pulled his pants up as he started to back out of the café, while he talked some shit. "I'm sure this won't be the last time we meet again."

The server put my club sandwich on the table and refilled my coffee, and before I took a bite, I said, "I'm positive, Jack!"

My eyes walked him out of the door and in his car until he drove off. Bobby didn't come across being the silent type so I assumed the obvious, realizing the pressure that I just put on him. It won't be long before he makes a move on me.

I continued to read my paper when the server voiced her concern, "I was worried for a minute, Lonnie. That man seemed very angry. Are you okay?"

"Just fine, sweetie; here's a better tip than the average. When a man is down and out, he can always count faithfully on two things, which are death and a loved one. However, when death is the only option, his loved one will always faithfully turn to someone he loves more."

I cautiously took a sip of my coffee before I continued, "Babydoll, to that chicken hearted, son-of-a-bitch you seen a minute ago, today was a revelation, but to Lonnie Biggs, it was just another Tuesday."

MICHAEL MCGREW

STANDING ON A GOOD FOOT
BUT WALKING ON A BAD LEG

I walked into the café with intentions to confront an issue, but wound up walking out confused, yet interested in the information that Lonnie
Biggs knew about me. I already knew that I
wasn't going to get anywhere with James if I even
spoke his name, so I took it upon myself to act as
judge and jury.

My mind was racing two hundred miles an
hour and I began to feel nauseous. The more I
thought about his reason to fuck with me, the
more intrigued I became about preventing it. I
knew only a little about him, and what I did
know, didn't help me at all. I felt trapped with no
way to start on my search for the facts, and it
was stressful because I had a lot to lose in a matter that concerned my well-being. I've never been
the one for games but in this case, it seemed
worth playing. I mean, it did involve my life.

For the first time in my life, I felt like an
unlocked door, unable to control the entry of my
surroundings and it scared me. Whom could I
really trust? Two hours into my confusion, I
found myself throwing down shots and drinking
myself sober, until things became quite clear
what had to be done. Lonnie had to die!

James and Jennifer returned from the Cayman Islands with unforgettable expressions on their faces.

142

In a way, I was excited that they were back, and even more excited to see Jennifer. I didn't mention my problems because it was pointless bringing them to the surface.

Being co-dependent has never been my forte, but since my release, my perception of James has genuinely been like big brother and it was starting to get old. He took care of me for six years, and now that I was out and facing a bigger problem, James turned a blind eye instantly.

I guess expecting someone to eliminate your worries is the same as watching water flow uphill; it is just not going to happen. James was ready to get back to the office to check the progress that we made; and it showed on his face that he was impressed. Our first meeting covered a lot of ground.

"Vgo D'artiste is complete with his album and it's a guaranteed classic," I commented.

"That's great! I just got off the phone with the VP of Hilton and we're negotiating a digital marketing campaign. So far they're interested in advertising our single," James updated.

"The digital age is here and we've got to conform to different ways of marketing to generate a buzz. If we don't have music rotating, then nobody's coming to see the artist perform," Damien said, and it made so much sense.

"And that's what we pay your firm the big bucks for. Our company needs to take it to the next level," James said.

I could feel the energy in the air and some real moves were about to be made. We needed a head-liner and because of that reason, Sydne Renee's project got pushed back because of the high-demand for Vgo D'artiste and his innovative style of music.

"Okay great. Gentlemen, see you next Tuesday. Always a pleasure," Damien said on his way out. The seats in the office were comfortable and I rested my head, before something came to mind that's been weighing heavy on my conscious.

"My position shouldn't have been looked at as a threat, man, this is our company and we've come a long way. Too long for you to think I'll compromise my integrity with you."

"I was just miserable, man. It was a dark period for me and I wanted someone to stoop down to my level for a second, that's all. But I thank you for being strong because I needed that, I love you and Jennifer for that and I mean that."

Like a spell has been cast, the sweet smell of Jennifer's Burberry Britt perfume took claim to my sense, taking me to a place as gratifying as breathing for the first time.

"I want this to last forever, Bobby; there's something about your eyes that drives me crazy," I heard Jennifer's voice say, and it was just as clear as when I thought I heard my mother's voice in prison. My dick was hard and it was so uncomfortable.

James was wrapping up his conversation and ready to leave. ". . . On my way to the house to get some sleep. Jennifer's in for a surprise tonight. I haven't been giving her the attention she needs, and I know she's been waiting patiently. Are you waiting for something or what?"

"No; why you ask that?" I replied, trying to cover up the fact that I was sexually aroused at the moment.

"Because you're still sitting down and nobody is here!"

"Oh nah, I'm just thinking about something, I'll catch you though," I said and James left in a hurry.

I called Stacy and told her to pick up some groceries, and headed home. Besides the bills, I was glad to get another letter from String, and he mentioned his release date. He wanted me to pick him up. I didn't write back because I was going to visit him the following weekend.

By this time, Stacy was showing pretty decent and getting moody, so I decided to pamper her by preparing some Oyster Rockefellers as a starter, while I cooked shrimp Alfredo and garlic bread with Colombian Crest wine to wash it down, topped with her favorite desert: chocolate covered strawberries.

Sitting there watching her helped me realize the seriousness of my future—and Stacy was just that—my future . . . my family . . . my heart. Stacy and I took a bath together and we relaxed, talked, and debated the name of our first-born son. I rubbed her stomach as our hands intertwined together as one.

I initiated a moment to express my love.

"I want our baby to have no worries, to never have to go to sleep hungry or ask you where I am. I want a family, baby, and I won't settle for any less than the happiness that I have with you. I love you, Stacy."

She turned around and smiled before handing me a towel to wash her back. She enjoyed these sentimental moments and took advantage as she voiced her opinion of me. "Bobby, I just hope that you never hurt me. I am all yours. You're my motivation, my appetite, and even my reason to look forward to the next day."

I washed her back while listening to her confession only to reflect on my own behavior. Here's a woman who put my life before her own. She was intelligent, outgoing, sexy and supportive, with a loving personality; everything that a nigga needed in his life. So why was I risking the future with my potential wife over a temporary crush? Simple, I haven't gotten caught yet.

She turned around and looked me in the eyes, reminding me of her alluring and seductive charm that enhanced her hidden purpose to prove to me that she was here to stay. Bubbles covered sections of her body as she rose with a look that would eliminate deny rejection. My dick joined in and rose, giving her appearance applause.

"Now don't start something you can't finish, girl."

"The only thing between us is air and opportunity," she said jokingly.

I looked up at her with a smirk and said, "Now that's gangsta!"

"Whatever."

"Quit talking and come here," I demanded.

"Yes, daddy."

Stacy's disposition announced that the freak was in the building. The water in the tub was midlevel; she knelt down grabbing my dick with both hands and helped me get it up to its fullest potential, before putting it in her mouth, consuming my buoy in our ocean of love. Her ass was in the air and she knew what the result of her good head would lead to, so I didn't expect it to last to long, and besides, her waxed, wet prized possession was calling me.

"All right, baby, stop and turn around. I want you to ride this dick until this bath water makes our fingers wrinkle."

Her ass spread wide and I think her bite-sized candy asshole winked at me.

"Oh, daddy, you feel so good in me. Baby, I love you."

"Damn, I love your ass!" Water was splashing and we were getting at it like rabbits until she smacked her head on the faucet.

"Oh shit, baby, you okay?" I asked.

She covered her right eye in embarrassing pain, only to realize instantly the gash above her eyebrow when she looked in the mirror. "Bobby, look at me, honey. Oh my God, I'm bleeding!"

She was hysterical and had a good reason to be, because a band-aid was out of the question; so I said, "Come on, baby, let's get dressed and go to the hospital."

I dampened a washcloth with warm water for her to cover her wound, and by the time we got to the hospital, it was full of blood. We checked into the emergency room and the wait was not short. When they finally called her to be seen, I decided to stay in the waiting room.

On my way to the soda machine, two cops approached me, "Hi, I'm Officer Buchanan and this is my partner, Officer Stanley; would you mind coming with us?"

"Sure, what's the problem?"

"We'll discuss all of that in a minute, but you'll need to come with us now, sir!"

I took my sweet time as I purchased my cola and followed them outside, immediately lighting a cigarette. "So what's up, gentlemen? My girlfriend is in there and I was just about to check on her."

"Well that's our concern and the primary reason why we were notified." I almost spit on the officer's uniform when he said that shit, and I knew he wasn't about to say what I thought he was.

"Whoa, whoa, let me see if I comprehend this clearly, you think that I did that to her? Officer, with all due respect, all bullshit to the left because ya'll ain't right for this shit. Go ask her if I did that to her and write that in your note pad."

"Sir, domestic violence cases are more common than murder. In fact, one hundred and seven women died as a result of domestic violence just last year, and thirty percent of the women in this emergency room are here because of injuries caused by abuse, so miss me with the bullshit that your talking. I didn't read you any Miranda rights and you're not under arrest. This is just routine, sir. We're just here to get some information and ask your spouse some questions, and everything will be fine, okay?"

"Yeah, whatever."

"How long have you been dating Ms.?"

"Stacy Nelson."

"Ms. Stacy Nelson; and how did she sustain her injury?"

"We've been dating a little over a year and she bumped her head on my twenty-three-hundred-dollar spa tub faucet."

"Have you ever been charged with domestic abuse in the past?"

"No."

"Do you have a license or identification card?" I gave him my license and he took my information down.

"Okay, thank you for your cooperation. We're just going to check out the information that you provided us with Ms. Nelson, and unless her story is different, then you have a good night."

Officer suck, and his partner, my dick, left, and I stayed outside until Stacy came out thirty minutes later. She gave me a look as if she was more embarrassed than hurt. I noticed her four stitches and told her that she was still beautiful. It cheered her up a little. Leaving the hospital was amusing as we reflected her near-death experience.

"Baby, what were the cops talking about?"

"Boo, those assholes were trying to convince me that you beat me or some shit! I was like, nah, it was an accident and they just left. I think they were disappointed. And even if you did do it, I wouldn't have snitched, I would've just shot yo' ass!"

"Boo, let's get out of here before you slip on a banana peel, and they try to charge me for that." We laughed as I opened the door for her, got in the car, and drove home. She was on medication and fell asleep shortly after we got there. I stayed up for a while watching her.

The past two years have had its difficulties, and a lot has changed. By now, Stacy was eight months pregnant with the baby shower around the corner, James was still doing coke, and String's release date was around the corner. The only difference was Jennifer and I had completely stopped using condoms.

In the beginning, we were seeing each other at least three times a week, and now we were only hooking up once a week. I felt the fire slowly turning into ashes and times were changing as our circle of friendship progressed.

James and Jennifer finally set a date for their wedding, and Stacy proposed to Jennifer, in front of everybody at the baby shower, for her hand in our son's life as his godmother. It got to the point where you didn't see one couple without the other; making holidays, vacations and those drawn-out movie nights the most difficult for me. The situation was too heavy and guilt was beginning to settle like the pilgrims on Thanksgiving.

I was on my way out of the house when my phone rang. I picked up the receiver and heard the automated voice say, *"This is Atlanta Federal Penitentiary with a collect call from String. If you accept these charges, please press one."* And I did.

"What's up, homie? Where you at?"

"The house, nigga! You only have the house number."

"I'm out, slim. I need you to pick me up. I told you I was getting out today."

"Man, I thought you were getting out next week. I'll be there in a minute."

On my way to pick him up, I stopped at one of my spots to purchase an outfit and some smokes as a warm-up gift. String was my boy and if I was on, then he was too. When I pulled up in the '09, he didn't know how to act.

"Oh shit, dog, it's like that!" I showed him his outfit and he couldn't wait to get in it.

"Man, that's that Gucci, huh? I'm in the game now, baby! It even smells expensive; my nigga, Bobby, got me smellin' like money! Whoa!" He was excited and just stood there. I had to snap him out of it; I didn't want to be in front of that prison no longer than I had to.

When we got into the car, String couldn't stop talking. "What's up, ace? Niggas be talkin' about ya'll in there, man, and I know tonight you gonna show me the town and everything, but I'm ready to get this paper. I need a position in your army and that's real!"

He passed me a short from his cancer stick and I accepted, taking a drag and continuing, "You already know, pimp, I got you! You got a place to stay, right?"

"Yeah, my peoples stay in Decatur," String replied.

"Well crash there until I get you a place of your own."

"Okay," he said.

"Well I hope you're well-rested because we're popping bottles tonight."

String has been waiting for this day for as long as I've known him, and I didn't let him down. All I had was one fucking favor to ask from him, to kill Lonnie Biggs! When we got to the house, we talked shit and swallowed spit for hours, until it was time to leave for the club.

He wasn't prepared for the world that I was going to introduce him to. He had an idea what level we were on but actually being there, and being acknowledged as a member of the team, was much different. His demeanor gave me a strong feeling that I couldn't be touched, and I felt secure. I almost knew right then what position I wanted him to hold down for the company, Vgo's personal security. I decided to tell him the next day.

James was proud to see me enjoy myself and mingle amongst the crowd when I was released from prison, and I felt the same way toward String. Passing down a blessing is worth living for, but unfortunately, my blessing had a price. The next day was a long one. String was like a debt collector when it came to the ladies—all over them! I can't recall myself ever being so horny in my life. He was getting at everything breathing, and despite his intentions to repopulate the world, he was excited about his new responsibility as the head of security.

James and I discussed String's agenda in full-detail over dinner and drinks at Lombardi's Restaurant. Vgo D'artiste joined in shortly after, and they clicked like brothers. After dinner, we sat and allowed our food to digest while we told jokes and reacquainted ourselves. String was coming around like he'd practiced these moments over the years. His presence was exceptionally respected and people were drawn to him, especially Sydne, but I wasn't having that at all, it would take a psychiatrist to get String out of her head. He wasn't shy and like most guys who are new on the street, he didn't have to worry about where his next meal was going to come from.

"James, I think I know you better than you know yourself. Bobby used to talk about you faithfully, G. I don't think you'll ever have to worry about this cat. Man, I can leave my wife and him alone in my house, and she could be naked, drunk off that Cisco, and ain't had none in years, and I still wouldn't think negative about this guy. This is my nigga and I trust him with my life," String screamed after a couple drinks.

"Yeah, he is one that you can trust; that's why he's my guy!" James replied.

I just sat there and listened to their compliments as they kept going on and on about their friendship with me; if they only knew that I didn't even trust myself at that time.

String continued with, "I remember I met him when he first got in the joint and I was like, 'This little pretty nigga ain't gonna last a minute in here,' but he proved me wrong once I found out that he knew more killas in there than I did; but I loved this dude the minute he spoke to me."

I couldn't stand to hear anymore of that shit, so I interrupted String's conversation for an important announcement. I called Vgo to come back to the table; he was getting at some ladies at the booth next to us. When he came back, I told everybody to raise their glasses and they did.

"This toast is to those who forgive the small mistakes, but never forget the big ones. Here's champagne for my real friends and real pain for my cham friends; my niggas, cheers!"

We downed our drinks and another before paying the tab and leaving. The ride home was very awkward because I kept thinking about what String had said at the restaurant, and it seriously bothered me. My efforts to justify my actions were useless, and I knew that James could never deceive me the way that I have him.

I dropped String off at his cousin's house so he could spend some time with his family, and on my way down the street someone called my name, and I stopped instantly to find out who it was. A kid pulled up on a motor scooter and started to make conversation.

"Damn, I knew you looked familiar, long time no see. The last time I saw you, you was at my daddy's house years back. It was you and your sister; she used to come to the house all the time, remember?"

I noticed what used to be a fresh R.I.P. T-shirt, but couldn't recognize the discolored face and it was pretty dark, but the name read: Melvin Biggs. Then I recalled my sister telling me at the Sundial about Millertime's son and me playing together. I wasn't sure, but figured I'd throw a name out there to get a reaction.

"Oh yeah, Millertime," I said with a little excitement.

"That's my pops; he was killed eight years ago. Yeah, I was young when he was murdered, but people be telling me stories about him all the time. How ya been?"

"Trying to get this money," I said, and I couldn't believe what I had just heard. It's funny how the truth comes to you as long as you stay focused and attentive.

I didn't have time for small talk and dove straight into asking him questions about the name on that shirt. "Are you related to a Lonnie Biggs?"

"Yeah, that's my grandfather."

I stared at the picture so hard that my pupils began to strain; and it all made sense to me why Lonnie Biggs wanted me walking on eggshells, and why James wanted me to stay away from him—I'd killed his son.

"It's a small world, man, but it's nice to see you again. Stay safe out here."

"You too, shawty," he replied.

I told the kid I had to leave and drove straight to the house to recollect the incident that just occurred. If only I'd seen where that kid came from, a portion of my problems could have been prevented. But at that time, it was the least of my concerns. Just the idea of knowing the reason behind Lonnie Biggs's impulsive actions toward me was gratifying enough. I still didn't know what cards he was holding, but I was just about to raise the stakes and my solution was just a phone call away.

"String, this is Bobby."

"What up, my nigga?"

"I got an itch that needs to be scratched and when it comes to this particular job, there are a few that we can trust. I know how it is when you get that taste of freedom, spending time with the family and all, but business is business and everything that we worked hard for is at stake; feel me?"

"Just write the letter and I'll read it, Bobby."

"Okay, I need someone to disappear."

"It's done."

"That's why I fuck with ya, dog! I'm gonna let you know though, okay?"

"That's what's up; now let me get back to this pussy, nigga! I'm out."

I was about to hang up when I heard him call my name. "What's up?" I said.

"Yo, why me?" String asked.

"Let's just say that you're the perfect guy for this one!"

MICHAEL MCGREW

ONE MAN'S LOSS
IS ANOTHER MAN'S GAIN

Thinking back, remembering conversations with String and his stories about his corrupt uncle, reminded me of the hate that manifested from his experience, and it opened my eyes to the golden opportunity that I was about to grant him by reintroducing them face-to-face. It was always those two initials that were branded internally in my brain; and when it all started to make sense, all I could appreciate was the time it took for the pieces to assemble. The Lonnie Biggs who harassed me was also the LB who neglected String as a child. String's uncle would soon be his target!

Situations were now filthy and my only motive was staying on top because it was too crowded on the bottom. It had been two weeks since Jennifer and I were together and I was ready to explode like a volcano, and that is when she called.

"Hey, you!"

I turned the volume up on my phone to hear her voice more clearly before I responded, "I was just thinking about you."

"So I guess like minds attract then, huh?" she said.

"I guess you can say that. I need to see you now and I'm not taking no for an answer!" I said. I was spoiled and was used to getting what I

158

wanted, the only time I didn't was when I was convicted.

Then Jennifer said, "Damn, Bobby, you know how much I need that miracle dick in me right now; and know how sexually incoherent your buddy is. I can't meet you just this minute, but I'll call you the moment I finish doing what I have to do, okay?"

I was slightly disappointed and felt overcame. She let it be known that I wasn't running anything but my mouth, but I was willing to play her game, and even though I had to wait for that pussy, it was fine with me. She had me open and when it came to Jennifer, I would have stood in line, and brought a lunch!

My phone beeped and it was my property manager complaining about a tenant, so I clicked back over to Jennifer, but she'd already hung up. To kill some time I decided to resolve the issue at the complex and hoped that she would call sooner than later, because I could tell she wasn't an En Vogue fan; holding on just wasn't her thing. When I got to the complex, I knew the problem was personal. When I pulled up, Raj, the property manager approached me.

"Mr. Williams, this is outrageous. The tenant in apartment number three is constantly harassing me and telling lies to my wife, and causing mischief and grief on us all. She must go this instant. I can't perform my duties under these conditions, please do something. Oh my God, here she comes!"

I looked to the left and noticed Denise, my homeboy's baby's momma, about to let the real story out and in the air for everyone to take in.

"Uh-uh, hell nah!! Tell him the whole truth, you fake-ass Mr. Marcus! All you talk about is porn and how you love Black women, you foreign freak."

Raj backed up and put his hands on his hips. "No, you shut the fuck up and go back home. You American women don't know when to stop talking. Just leave now and get the crunk out of here!"

Denise ignored him and put her hand in his face to talk to me.

"Bobby, you know me and I have never lied to you, right? Ever since Terrence went to jail, money has been tight and my rent has been short as an ant dick! This mothafucka here told me that he'd take care of me until things got better for me, and I don't think I have to tell you what he wanted in return, do I?"

"She's a lie, she's a lie," Raj exclaimed.

I've known Denise since we were knee-high to a fire hydrant, and she knew better than to run game on me. Raj was trying to abuse his power. He was busted and couldn't control himself, so I told him to let her finish and she did.

"I just found out that I was pregnant with his child and now he wants to kick me out. The kids and I don't have anywhere else to go . . ."

She went on and on about her fucking predicament. It wasn't that I didn't care about her situation, but in the midst of listening and deliberating like some circuit court judge, I dozed off and started thinking about Jennifer. She was similar to a drug, and I needed a fix as quick and promising, as a healthy heart needing a beat.

I grew a hard-on just thinking about her phone call, giving me the drop on where to meet her. I just wish it wasn't so obvious that my attention was elsewhere. I mean, there I was trying to settle a dispute, with my dick harder than Superman's kneecap. I couldn't make a decision about Raj right then and there, without consulting with James, but I already had it in my mind to fire him, and in return, hire Denise as his replacement. I told her not to worry about being homeless, and that being said, Raj understood that around here, we stuck together.

On my way to vacuum my car out, I ran into an old friend and pulled my phone out to save his number when I noticed three missed calls. My fucking phone was on silent mode the whole time. After I took his number, I returned the calls, two were from business partners and the other was from the Sheraton, I was connected to room number 202.

Jennifer was glad to hear from me and I was impatiently waiting to touch her. By this time I felt like I was being forced by nature, as guilt began to dilute my inappropriate expectations. When I got off the elevator, a woman said with a soft voice, "God bless you." I paused with a sharp pain that reminded me of acid reflux before smiling, letting her know that I appreciated her gesture.

The elevator door closed, as I stood alone, staring down what appeared to be the longest hallway, with a feeling that only a death-row inmate could relate to on that last walk down the corridor. When I got to the door I turned my phone off and fixed my collar to my Crooks N Castle T-shirt. Before I knocked, I hesitated numerous times; constantly thinking about leaving, considering that I still had time to decline my expected invite, but why? To repair what little integrity I had left? I am still a good friend and to those who would call me a dog, I'm not; I'm more like relationship's pet who enjoys biting more than just its owner, and on the other side of that door awaited an experience that angels could testify to the moment they entered the gates of heaven.

Fuck it!

I knocked three times with an aggression that only I could take notice to. Jennifer opened the door in a hot pink Victoria Secret mesh halter baby-doll and golden brown locks, resembling Blu Cantrell, only hotter, with no panties and all the qualifications to turn me the fuck out! She looked me up and down and squinted her eyes with a suspicion that a cop gives an underaged drinker, before saying, "You had me worried, hun. I've been jogging in place just waiting for you to melt in this pussy."

She let me in, turning around and walking toward the bathroom, before leaning on the doorframe, turning her head and facing me. The room was illuminated by candlelight; she threw her hair back and smiled before arching her back and exposing her ass cheeks as they peeked under her lingerie. She looked so good I could get packs of cigarettes just telling this story!

"I'm glad you could come, sweetness, you don't know how much this means to me. Get comfortable, baby. It'll only be a half of a minute before show time."

She shut the bathroom door behind her, leaving me to myself for a minute to elaborate on her remark, what's so different about this time that makes it so important than the others? It kept me guessing and it was something about that comment that lead me to believe that this was our last encounter together as one, so I took time to cherish every second of it.

Her half of minute was up so I occupied myself by undressing, until I was distracted by her overnight bag. I grabbed it with curiosity that reminded me of a stalker, finding myself with her blouse in my hand and under my nose. Her scent intoxicated me, disabling any incentive to let her go that easy. The bathroom door opened and the light revealed my obsessive act. Jennifer took some time killing the light as she stood there, enjoying the view of my naked muscular body sitting on the edge of her comfortable queen-sized bed. I tossed her blouse on the floor and stood up, looking her in those pools of warmth that we call eyes. My weapon was so hard and long, I probably would have had to register it if I was traveling, and if my body was used to tell time, it would be standing at a solid twelve-fifteen.

She turned off the light and walked toward me. I leaned, putting all of my weight on my right foot while rubbing my stomach, deliberately giving her the impression that I was starving for her sugar. She grabbed my left arm, backed into me like a wholesaler parking her goods to dock the merchandise, and I held her tight while she applied her cheek to my bicep, caressing my arm with her face like a kitten taking to its master.

 I turned her around and she gave me an acquisitive yet, anxious look that told me that she trusted me in great faith to revive the life of an orgasm that lives inside her pussy, and only makes appearances when I came around. Her lips were therapeutic to my needs and her body heat was identical to our moment of passion, hot! Both of us were thirsty with intent to please each other. Neither of us was happy to settle for sloppy seconds, so we sixty-nined until we both blew like Dizzy Gillespie's trumpet. My soldier was still at attention and ready for the order.

She licked all of the cum off of my mushroom and let it air-dry before mounting on it and riding it reverse cowgirl, constantly impaling herself with her head buried between my legs like a deep secret. I could barely keep my eyes open, but watching her ass shake and vibrate was like viewing a solar eclipse—it was memorable.

She stopped, looked at me and said, "Baby, you need to hit this from the back. Come on, daddy, and make me run from you."

I got on my knees as she positioned herself for doggy-style, and I paused to look at what I perceived as perfection before spreading her backyard doors open and eating her fresh fruit from her strawberry patch. I felt her hand on top of my head and her moans met my standard of gratification.

"Yes, baby, right *there*. Oh shit, Bobby! Oh, Bobby!!"

Her voice turned me on even more increasing my stamina. I went from side to side, round and round, down and, yes—up! My tongue was acquainting both of her holes. Bobby Williams was wide open and proud of it.

"Come inside me, baby," she said. I put it in slow and we both inhaled deeply with a satisfaction that virgins could never come close to. One of my legs were up, giving me room to penetrate deep inside her as she received every inch of my groomed penis. The deeper I went, the more her walls spread, sounding off with a noise comparable to a Whoopee Cushion. She grabbed my hand, redirecting me to pull her hair; her head snapped back when I pulled it, she yelled, "Yes!" and then she proceeded to play with herself.

We switched positions from the side to missionary and ended up on the edge of the bed, sitting up with her legs wrapped around me, grinding slow and breathing hard. All I could do was smile in appreciation of what my double life had to offer. The whole room smelled like good sex; a fragrance so attractive, if I could bottle it, P. Diddy would get jealous. My head began to get hot so I picked Jennifer up while I was still in her, laying her on her back. We kissed as a couple before subjecting to the reality that a relationship on that level, would never occur, but separating completely would be harder than imagined.

We continued to allow our fantasy to play to the finish. I stroked her with emotion, putting my head past hers and into the pillow that she lay on. I went fast and slow, deep, and even toyed with her by pulling out, eating her, and jabbing it back in until . . ., "Oh my God, honey, I'm about to cum! Her eyes rolled and she grabbed her breast.

She went crazy, biting her lip and covering her face with her hands. She screamed in a pleased tone and I went faster and faster until I pulled out to cum on her stomach. As I ejaculated, Jennifer came non-stop. It was like nothing I've ever seen. A rich flow of liquid was coming out of her as I began to panic, before I remembered my sister telling me that when two people understand each other, physically and mentally, it creates a feeling so strong that it becomes uncontrollable, and when that connection reaches its peak, you'll recognize right then if a woman is weak for you.

We sat there motionless with looks of our future in question, and the little time we spent looking at each other confirmed my beliefs that neither of us were as resilient as I initially thought. We were at our last stop, with separate directions, and right then, I noticed how relevant she was in my life, and how special that experience was to us.

We made a connection that prioritized my excuse to keep her around, we manipulated time and made it work in the likeness of a thrill, and at the end of the day, it is what it is, that night we made love. It was hard to understand that I was intimate with someone whom I was restricted to love at all.

I showered with no soap and changed my voice mail to its original greeting before I left. Leaving the hotel was a lot easier than coming, and when I walked out, I took in the breeze, lit a cigarette, and tipped the valet before hightailing it to the house. Passing all those restaurants made my mouth water. I walked into my house hungry as hell, but was temporarily sidetracked when I heard laughter inside of my den. I entered the room to see what was going on, until I heard Stacy say, "Hey baby, I left a message on your voice mail. Shouldn't you just buy a new battery? How would you know if I started to give birth if your battery is always dead? These are some friends from my Lamas class."

She dug into a bowl of what appeared to be popcorn while lifting a paper drawing before continuing with, "We-uh, bunch of pregnant bitches, just playing Pictionary. Everybody, this is my oldest son, Bobby."

Everybody laughed and I waved before I dashed for the kitchen to prepare my favorite entrée: a bacon, egg, and cheese sandwich; when James called and told me to meet him outside. I couldn't fucking believe it! I just got in the house and I knew Stacy was going to bitch if I turned around and left again. I didn't even want to walk past the den, but I did.

"Hey, baby, I'll be back in a minute. My phone is upstairs charging, so if you need me, then call James. I'll be with him, okay?"

"You just got here, baby."

"I know, baby, I don't know what the fuck he wants me for and I don't plan on being too long, please believe it! Did you rent the movie?"

"Five Heartbeats, right?"

"Yeah, and by the time ya'll finish that boring-ass game, I should be back. And ya'll should watch Stacy because she cheats!"

"Get outta here, boy!" Stacy giggled.

When I got outside James was already in front. When I approached the car, he opened the door from the inside.

"I need you to take a ride with me right quick."

I got in and we drove off. It was total silence between the both of us; the type of silence that would alarm the conscious of the guilty, but my sense of smell took control of my attention. There was a very familiar scent in the air, but I couldn't put my finger on it at that point.

We stopped at a red light before turning into a fast food restaurant parking lot, a couple of blocks from the house.

James turned the car off and continued to look straight while he spoke, "My main man, Bobby. I know it's been a lot going on and we haven't had a chance to talk, so what's up, brotha?"

Shit, we could've had this conversation at the house. "Nothing, man; just business as usual, same shit, different flies, you know. So what's—"

James interrupted me with a frustrated voice. "So you and Lonnie Biggs had a lunch date recently, huh?"

He finally looked at me with eyes that gave me a clear notification that I had trespassed against him, but it was something about that scent.

I responded with, "Man, go ahead, James, this nigga is fucking with me for unknown reasons and you expect me to do nothing about it! You ain't giving me any answers, so I started asking the questions, and now that I know everything that I need to know to stay ahead of the game like I'm supposed to, little Lonnie is about to get a pop quiz." I had James's full attention when I told him that I was aware of some things about Lonnie Biggs. His demeanor changed as if I touched a nerve. He began to ask questions, "What do you mean everything?"

"I know that Lonnie Biggs is up to something because I killed his son, but I'm also confused about him not doing anything about it."

"Millertime was his son?" he said with a surprised look.

"Flesh and blood. It's a small world isn't it, dog?"

"Damn! So you gonna take care of him?"

"Like a bad itch, homie; so why were you acting all funny and shit, like you were gonna take me to a field and whack me, or something?"

"I've just been having a lot on my mind and hearing about your run-in with that snake just didn't sit right with me. I know I've been avoiding that subject, but I don't wanna ruin my day talking about him. And you need to understand that it's best if you just leave him the fuck alone. You're my nigga and the closest one to me besides, Jennifer, and that gives me more reasons to be on a need-to-know basis—and anything concerning him, I need to know! Feel me?"

I rolled down the window to get some air. "I got you."

James's phone rang and I started to glare at the traffic that passed by when it finally hit me, that scent on Jennifer's blouse, in her bag, was the same exact scent that greeted my nose when I entered James car. I remembered her important business that came before me when I asked to see her earlier; and there is nothing more important than spending quality time with your future husband. That bitch had his smell on her when I got to the room, and that's why she went to the bathroom when I got there, she fucked me after she served her king!

James turned on the car in an obvious hurry before trying to end the call. "Okay, we're on our way."

He hung up the phone and put the car in reverse before telling me that Stacy was going into labor. When I got to the house we took her to the hospital and I was hysterical about my son coming into the world.

Everything was fine until her legs opened and the doctor started to give directions. I realized right then that I was in for a long night, and wasn't going anywhere for a while. The nurse asked me where I was going and I replied with, "To get a snickers bar!"

THE BIRTH OF DESTRUCTION

"Okay, Ms. Nelson, I'm going to need you to relax. I think you're contracting now because this baby is coming, okay?" the doctor said.

"Good job, honey," I said with an encouraging feel.

The doctor started the procedure.

"Push—1-2-3-4-5-6-7-8-9—push."

The doctor continued as the assistant and I comforted her.

"How do you feel, baby?" I asked.

"How the hell do you think I feel, Bobby? *You* try having a baby out of *your*—Oh, shit! Get this baby out of me, please!"

"Okay, Mr. Williams, if you wouldn't mind continuing with your cycle, helping to comfort her, please. She needs all the support she can get right now, sir."

I held Stacy's hand and padded sweat from her forehead. She didn't want anyone else in the room but us, making it harder on me and my patience, because I wasn't going to be too many assholes.

"Push, young lady, I don't want to hear any loud noises or crying. Just direct all of that energy down here to the bottom, okay?"

"Yeah!" Stacy answered back.

"Okay, we're going to have the baby next time. I just have to make a little more room and that should be it, okay? It should be the next one and you will be able to blow it out, young lady. Next time you have a contraction, you will be bringing your beautiful son into the world. It's about to be birthday time!"

Stacy looked at me and said, "Tell me you love me, Bobby. I need to hear it."

"I love you, baby. You're doing great."

"I just want to push it out, baby."

The nurse advised Stacy to be calm, as she said, "No, Ms. Nelson, save your energy and just wait for the next contraction. It's a lot of pressure because the baby is here."

"Okay." Stacy began to push and scream and scream and push with her head unable to stay still, and her eyes closed shut.

"There he is; lots of hair. Here he comes."

"It's almost over, baby," I said.

"Oh, yes! HAPPY BIRTHDAY!" the doctor said.

The baby cried easing our tension. The doctor lifted him up for Stacy to view before wiping him off, and it was recorded that our son was born at eleven fifty-two. After I cut the umbilical cord, the doctor handed him to his mother, and I kissed them both on the head before the doctor asked, "So, do you have a name for this handsome devil?"

Stacy looked at me before responding to the question and said, "Bobby . . . Bobby Williams, Jr."

I couldn't wait to relay the news to our loved ones in the waiting room.

"It's a boy!" I screamed, and everybody was just as happy as I was, except James, who seemed bothered. A couple of people went into the delivery room to see Stacy and Bobby Jr. while I sat and talked to James.

"I'm one up on ya, playa, and I know that ain't what you frowning about, so what's up?"

"Have you heard from Jennifer? I was with her earlier and haven't heard from her since. I think something's wrong, man. I've never gone this long without at least talking to her. Her phone is going straight to voice mail and I even left messages letting her know about her new godson. I don't mean to rain on your parade, Bobby, but something just isn't right. However, I'm happy for you. I truly am. I just can't control my emotions, and I apologize."

"I'm pretty sure she'll call you later, don't stress. She loves you, dog."

I left to go back to spend the rest of my night with my family, leaving James alone and confused. I can't imagine the thoughts that jogged through his mind. Stacy's uncle caught a glimpse of his ill-temperament on his way to the soda machine. James paced foolishly until he stormed out of the hospital. I was concerned about him and it was the wrong time for him to be alone, but the timing was just terrible for me to be a dependable friend.

I spent the next three days with Stacy and the baby to get things established at home. On the fourth day, I went to check on James since I hadn't heard from him. When I pulled up to his house that afternoon, I noticed his car, so I knew he was home. When I walked up the steps, I picked up his daily newspapers; there was four altogether.

The door was unlocked so I walked in, only to meet the acquaintance of an unattractive stench. The only availability for light was what his custom wood blinds allowed through the cracks. I opened them to let some life into what used to be a happy home, only to see James lying on the couch. He covered his eyes with an attitude that made me feel unwelcome before correcting himself in an upright position.

James mumbled, with sure confidence that his wish had come true, "Jennifer."

When he noticed that love had delivered another low blow, he continued, "Ah, shit, Bobby, what's up?"

"Damn, James, are you all right? You look bad, man." I started to itch just being around him, so I started to pick up random trash that took claim to his surroundings. He looked vulnerable and beat, and at that moment, I learned that if you want to defeat a man, you have to work him from the inside.

Never in a hundred years did I think that I would ever come to envision a depressed version of James. A man with a mysterious passion and a will to pursue goals to prove to more than just himself, that anyone can grab the success stick and run with it, but with every strength lies a weakness, and his, unfortunately, was reliability. I stared at James and his attempts to get together.

He took a drink before hovering over his glass coffee table to snort a line of coke.

"Did you come here just to tell me that shit, Bobby?"

"Damn, I mean you don't answer your phone, so I'm coming to check on ya."

"Well I just had a lot to deal with and needed to be alone. I'm coming back to the office on Monday."

"Nigga, it's Thursday! You need to get out of this . . . whatever that you're in."

James got up and stumbled to the window before catching his balance to stare outside of his front room window, like an after-school kid expecting his mother's presence to meet his eye, but in this case, never.

James began to speak, "Bobby, she's not coming back; everything she owned is gone except her engagement ring and cell phone. She didn't leave a letter or even contact information for me to reach her again. I don't know why, Bobby; she was everything to me and I thought I was to her, but obviously I assumed wrong. The darkness is where I belong, man. I feel like a part of me has vanished.

"I've been up for days and seen numerous sunrises, thinking about love and the meaning of it. I used to think love was a pick up on the first ring, or those shameless expressions we give, assuring our satisfaction for each other; overlooking the small things to focus on the big picture, with bedroom promises and daytime secrets. Love is growing old together with memories to laugh at during breakfast. It sounds good doesn't it, Bobby?"

He turned to me awaiting a response, his eyes told me that he no longer believed anything that he said, but still needed to know if love still existed in anyone else's heart besides his own. I chose not to interfere with his anguish. My heart was beating so hard as I felt his pain. I probably wouldn't have even been able to hear myself speak.

James continued, "And, I was wrong, Bobby." He laughed. "Love . . . you wanna know about love—love is an infection that spreads at a speed undetermined by emotion. First, it locates the eyes and uses them as a puppet to lead it to its supervisor, which is the brain. Once the love's attraction has met the brain's requirement through the eye, it is later introduced to the owner and CEO, which is the heart. Love later sets in, infiltrating, confusing and misleading both the brain and the heart, causing conflict between them as the eyes manifest guilt, losing their confident outlook as the transition began fresh and healthy, but ended up tired, sad and frustrated. Now with old eyes, a programmed brain, and a bruised heart, a once charismatic and prideful man becomes a product of his own fear, and his company collapses with a bitter taste in his mouth to remind him everyday about the love that led him astray.

"Love is an unmarked grave in a cemetery surrounded around the lonely. It is a piece of candy wrapped with a ribbon and celebrated once a year. It's a curse, a red flag, and a flagrant foul. Love is two people feeling sorry for each other."

I was lost for words when I heard his new description and couldn't help but partially blame myself. But as long as Jennifer was gone I didn't have to worry about it getting worse.

I couldn't let him go out like this so I said, "James, you have the right to feel the way you do, but how long will this go on? I can't tell you anything that will make you feel better, but I will say this for damn sure, you got to get over this hump playa. You're better than this, James, and you got to think more positive. I'll pick up the slack for two weeks so you can get your shit together, but you got to get better. Do you think Jennifer is sitting around depressed and shit?"

"Man, I don't want to live anymore."

"Do you have a closet in your pocket?"

"What?"

"Because you need to hang that bullshit up, James! Don't be talking like that; you've got a lot to live for and this can be overcome."

I finished cleaning up and talked to James a little more before I left. James was really hurt, but I knew he would get over it, and besides, it was time to prep String for his big job. Since he was fresh out of the penitentiary, and friends with a convict, I felt it was necessary to get him involved with projects to increase his status in the company, to establish friends in case his character would ever raise suspicion.

I'd had no more run-ins with Lonnie since the café incident, but I didn't underestimate him at all. He was following me, and might have even known more than I thought he did. I knew he was up to something and I was eager to beat him to the finish line. But in order for things to go smoothly, everything had to go as planned; and what better timing to arrange the hit than the night of Vgo D'artiste's performance at the Phillips Arena in our hometown.

It would take two months to get it all configured. The timeframe between my plot and the concert was perfect. String would be on the books to prove his employment with the company. Now being a tax-paying citizen, loved and respected by his co-workers, and not having any run-ins with the law, it would be hard to point the finger in his direction. His alibi would be solid during the time the murder was supposed to take place, considering he would be working as the headliner's security at the concert.

I thought I had all the corners covered and my sixty-day master plan to eliminate Lonnie Biggs called for a celebration, but instead, that night I went home to my family. In the streets, I could easily mask my emotion; it came natural because of the shit that I dealt with on a daily basis, it was a survival tactic, but in my own home, vulnerability was written all over my face.

I sat on the couch to catch the last twenty minutes of the news, and Stacy approached me from behind, kissing me on the cheek. A sharp feeling jolted through my body as it quickly turned an uneasy frown upside down. I grabbed her and she fell on my lap as we cuddled and continued to kiss. I slid my hand under her bed shirt and I was getting ready to take her upstairs, until she reminded me of her provision. Oh my God! Those six weeks was killing me! Therefore, we wound up doing what I'm pretty sure she enjoyed at that time more than I. We talked, and that was the last night that I can remember that I slept well.

Two months later . . .

Since my release, I had watched and participated in the growth of a company so unique and successful, than I never thought in my days of becoming a hip-hop mogul. Like Russell Simmons had LL Cool J, or Damon Dash had Jay Z, Vgo D'artiste was our ticket—our MVP, and biggest investment! He was going to make history with his performance, and his double-platinum record was promising. The "My Kinda Girl" single was the perfect track that was going to give us commercial status, and everyone was going to be talking about this event. There was only two days before the concert and my two-month plan was in its final chapter. I was forty-eight hours away from closure to at least one of my issues, considering I haven't gotten over Jennifer's disappearance, but Lonnie Biggs's death, I figured, would compensate for her absence.

It kind of bothered me that it's been two months since I'd seen James. He was conducting business over the phone in conference meetings, and left the groundwork for me. I didn't bother even tracking him down anymore and wasn't going to babysit him, neither, but I knew he was at least going to attend the concert.

I called String to give him the run down and he was with Vgo and the program director at the arena. "What up, Bobby?"

"Ain't shit, what you doin?"

"Chillin' with Vgo, and getting things straight for Thursday."

"Well Thursday is the day and everything is everything. Now check me out, String, after our meat is cooked, we really gonna eat, you follow me? If you pull this off, you're set, playa."

"It is what it is," String said calmly.

"I'm gone. Tell Vgo I said don't freeze like no bitch!"

He laughed, "I'll do that." When I hung up my phone, I noticed my son's face as a screensaver. Stacy must have put it on there before I woke up that morning. It made me want to go home and I almost did, but Magic City was going down and I wasn't gonna miss it that night. I wasn't really the strip club type, but you would've thought Obama was in the building. The girl at the front window was acting as if she didn't know me, asking for ten dollars and shit.

"I don't have ten dollars. Where's the owner?"

"He ain't here; you can't get everywhere with those good looks, sorry, next!"

"Baby, I'm far from broke. I don't pay to get in no joint in my own town. Where you from?"

"A little town called ten dollars cheapskate! Are you a registered citizen?"

I pulled out my five-thousand-dollar stack and said, "Here smart ass, bust that." I gave her a hundred-dollar bill and told her to let the other nine people in for free, before giving her a business card. When she recognized whom she was disrespecting, I was already past the curtain. I'm pretty sure she heard the DJ announce my name when I entered. I went straight to the bar for a double shot of "top shelf" when a familiar voice asked me if I wanted to request a song. When I turned around, I noticed it was that stink-bitch Coco.

"Getting some head by Shawna, something that you can relate to!" I said, taking a napkin from her tray to wipe my mouth. I balled the napkin and tossed it back on the tray. She frowned out of embarrassment.

"How's your car, nigga?" she asked.

"So you're the one who trashed my car? Fuck is wrong with you, Coco?" I replied. This was new to me, all the time I thought it was Lonnie Biggs.

"That's what happens when you play with women's hearts, you lame-ass nigga."

"No, that's what I get for dealing with a local! Get out of my face before it becomes an issue ho!" She tried to kiss me and I had to push her face. It was so embarrassing to see how desperate a woman can act at times.

"You know what, fuck you, Bobby!" she screamed. She spilled a drink on my shirt and stormed off, and I was glad that it had finally ended—hopefully.

I headed to the bathroom and called James when I entered, but I got no answer. He called me back while I was leaving a message, and when I switched over I asked, "Damn, nigga, you don't fuck with me no more?"

"What? Turn that shit down, I can't hear you; are you at the club?"

"I'm at Magic City, come through, it's live but you probably still grieving with yo' punk ass!"

"Fuck you; I'm on my way."

He seemed to be getting a little better with his social life. Me, personally, the only way I could've gotten over a female would be to sleep with another; but not James, he enjoyed being with himself as if he were damaged goods.

"Hey, order whatever you want, man, it's about time you got out. You're beginning to develop a habit of disappearing, what's up with that?"

"I had to fall back, man, and get me together ya know, you can't enjoy what you've worked hard for if you're not healthy, right?"

"I feel you on that, and that's the first thing we're going to toast to—health!" He paid for a couple lap dances and he was acting like a virgin, but I could tell that he was getting his swagger back.

I didn't stay too long, though, because I needed to focus on Thursday. I couldn't really sleep that night and stayed up with the baby most of the night, but I know Stacy rested peacefully and that's what counts.

Thursday . . .

A necessary sacrifice was going to be made for the sake of our companies future, as well as Vgo D'artiste's explosive performance and release of our new hit single "My Kinda Girl", to prove that Good Game Records was hip-hop's grandchild, and that is why this day was so important. I'd waited two months for this day, and I believed to the core of my soul that it was fail proof.

The concert was at eight that night but Vgo was to perform at nine. Everything was organized, from the sound check to the after party, and all the staff knew their place, except the most important pawn in my twisted scheme—String. He met me at my house, still unaware of who the target was, but eager to put in work to secure his position in my army. I gave some added responsibility to some interns, giving me extra time to see things through, until it was time for me to head back to the arena. It was eight-thirty when I drove String to the scene, a familiar landmark to us both—the precinct.

String gave me an odd look and said, "What are we doing here, dog?"

I pointed to Lonnie Biggs's black Crown Victoria and said, "The person who drives that car right there has been a thorn in my fucking hip and a serious threat to our progress; and when I needed this job done I knew it had to be someone I could trust and that person is you. I need you now to hold me down, you feel me?"

String looked me in the eyes before putting on his gloves and took the revolver from my hands, saying, "I got you, homie."

I looked outside my window and the office lights in the back were still on. I didn't want to spoil the surprise and wanted to hurry and get out of there, so I told String, "He should be coming out very shortly and when he does, I want you to put two in his head as soon as he attempts to get into his car. And when you do, drop the gun, and there's a car just one block away for you to drive back to the arena. It's a blue Magnum; here's the key.

"If you do this right, then you don't have any worries. When you see me at the arena, don't bother handing me the keys, they're yours now!"

I threw him the keys before asking him, "Are you straight?"

"Yeah, and if I miss Vgo's performance, I'm gonna kill yo' ass next!" We both laughed before he got out.

I drove off slowly as I watched String position himself behind a dumpster, preparing himself for the perfect murder. On my way to the arena, I lit my Romeo & Juliet cigar, anticipating seeing the outcome of everything.

When I was seated, I was no longer tense as I relaxed and took a couple of deep breaths, while sipping my Hennessy. I remember pouring a little for my sister and mother, but if I knew then what I know now about String, I would've poured the whole fucking bottle!

LONNIE BIGGS:
The Confrontation

It was a long night at the office and I was fuck-ing beat, but any night wouldn't be one with-out Candy; a whore from the eastside who likes it rough and hard like a true bitch is supposed to. I met her when she was just sixteen, a runaway with dreams that she couldn't reach if she was ten-feet tall, with an ass that would interrupt a bishop's speech; a bona fide student of the art in selling seduction for a negotiable fee.

My little pet is how I refer to her when we are together. I taught her the streets, lacing her boots about the game and how to play it without remorse; now she's a twenty-six-year-old woman with victories under her belt, and probably the closest person to this old heart of mine.

Her stepfather was a heavyset fella and wasn't your average Joe from the street. He'd been around the block, and had the scars to prove it; especially the deep one on his face that you'd think would prevent him from ever getting ass again. He was a forklift operator and breadwin-ner of the family, but was forced on disability when he sustained a massive back injury. He turned to alcohol to treat his pain and pride, but it didn't take too long for him to begin to focus more on Candy's curves, and make grotesque passes at her with sick perverse intentions to lick her jolly rancher.

Soon he began to rape and threaten her to never speak of what went on in that house, and with mommy forced to pick up another job to cover daddy's slack, she was never there to discontinue her daughter's early reconfiguration into adulthood. He allowed his deadbeat buddies to have their way with her for a small price, and even shared his profit with her, letting her know that there was more where it came from.

When Candy was suspended from school for prostituting herself in the bathroom, her mother was notified and she was forced to confess the horrible truth of her scandalous activities, that she was then calling her family business, which involved her stepfather.

He was arrested and sent to Atlanta Federal Penitentiary for his second offense and that found him in even deeper trouble once his record came back as a registered offender in another state. His prior convictions got him twenty years, and his violent crimes didn't help his situation either. Candy's mind was already corrupted, and even though she was free from her stepfather's control, her nose still smelt the blood of the tricks that circled the track.

When I asked her how she got her name, she told me that when her step daddy used to enter her room, he used to ask her if she wanted some candy. We became more than just intimate, and

I'd even paid her step daddy a visit to make things crystal clear to him. Before I left, he understood that he owed me a favor if he wanted to continue living in my house! The most important thing to me that night before seeing Candy, was what I had in my hand: Some very incriminating information that was left in my possession.

My deed regarding my delivery might not be considered a good one, but it for damn sure put a smile on my handsome face. I placed the twenty-two by twenty-seven jumbo manila envelope in the outgoing mail, and sent it to a Mr. Bobby Williams, 2312 E. Glynn Road, Atlanta, GA 30930. I'm through with these games and it was time to set-up my power move, burying the truth in his heart and letting it eat through his soul.

I looked at my watch and couldn't believe that it was eight forty-five, but I was happy it was Thursday. I put in some vacation leave for two weeks, and tomorrow is my last day. After I grabbed my coat, I headed to the door and the annoying sound of Detective Jones polluted my eardrum.

"Hey, Biggs, if I catch you breaking the law during your vacation, so to speak, I'll have to bring your black ass in early."

Detective Jones was a cracker who couldn't think past A—the epitome of ignorant. The type that lives in the past and is still upset about integration, and even though he worked with them, in the back of his mind, he always thought that we were all better off as slaves.

I couldn't stand him, and always fucked with his ego when I got a chance.

"The only thing I'll be breaking is your blonde haired, blue-eyed, chocolate-chip-cookie-baking, chocolate-dick-eating wife's back, jack!"

His face turned red but he knew he couldn't fuck with me, but he kept trying. He was stuck in his ways, so nobody took him seriously.

"Boy! You couldn't fuck my Susie if you fell into her cunt, jack!"

And I replied with, "Man, I can skydive blindfolded and land deep in some pussy, Detective; now don't you have some coffee to brew or something?"

"Fuck you, Biggs!"

"Yeah, two dicks don't stick, chump."

I left and decided to take the stairs while I called Candy.

"Hey, daddy,"

"How's my sexy pet?"

"Purring for you, baby. Where are you?"

"Leaving the precinct. I'll be there in a few."

"Well the streets are congested because of the concert tonight, so you should take the highway, it would be quicker."

"Yeah, well, get in the shower, I'll be there in a—" When I was opening the car, I heard someone behind me with an intimidating tone.

"Get the fuck off the phone and don't move."

I hung up on Candy and put my hands up, with my back still turned, and started to identify myself. "I'm a cop, son, and you don't want the law's blood on your hands. You think your life is rough now?"

He didn't respond so I turned around slowly to look him in the eyes, and the first thing I noticed was the barrel of his revolver. The second thing I noticed was the aged, but familiar face of the asshole behind the gun. It was a good night for a crime, and when the Lord called me, I promised him I wouldn't complain; and always told myself to welcome my death and greet it with a smile, so I did.

"Long time, nephew."

Xavier was shocked, and my first impression of his gesture was that it wasn't intentional for us to meet under these circumstances, until he spoke, "Uncle Lonnie? What the fuck!" He breathed heavily and seemed agitated by his thoughts, as if confused or mislead.

He held the bridge of his nose with his thumb and index finger. I approached him slowly to retrieve his piece, but he gripped it hard and pointed it with sure intent kill. When he focused himself, I saw a different man—a killer—and then he spoke, "You left me to die, man. I was only twelve. You could've stopped it. They tortured me for hours and treated me like I was some insect. They say blood is thicker than water, but you need water to live, and if killing you is gonna get me right with Bobby, then cheers, nigga!"

Mentioning Bobby's name triggered my own anger, "Bobby who; Bobby Williams? That piece of shit! Put the fucking gun down and let me tell you something now! We're blood, so put the fucking gun down before you make a mistake; will you listen to me, god dammit! My sister is your mother so put the fucking gun down. Do you know who the hell I was back in the day, and how many people wanted me dead?

"I couldn't come up with that kind of money unless I took it from my superiors, and if I couldn't pay it back, I would have buried more than my nephew. When I found out that you lived, didn't we take care of it?

"Tell me you didn't get a rush from seeing those animals tossed out onto the freeway like some old video game. You know you are an accessory to that crime, don't you son? You've got to understand, Xavier, that when you're in a high position in life and doing business with powerful people, one sacrifice is easier to swallow than ten. I'm sorry you had to go through that, nephew. Now put down the gun."

He lowered his gun and I had his full attention as I continued, "Don't you know Bobby killed your first cousin? Now he wants to kill me because I know all about James and his cover-ups; tracing back to his illegal business operations that funded the company."

Xavier obviously wasn't prepared to hear that, and was heated.

"That nigga killed Marlin—my ace?"

"I ain't the one you need to be pointing that gun at, boy." He put the gun in his waistband and backed up before leaving.

I called him, "Hey, nephew, for all that it's worth, I'm glad to see that you're okay."

He didn't respond as he continued to jog down the street. I opened my car door and got in to rest my head on the steering wheel, and reflect on the incident that had just taken place with Xavier. The last time I saw him was when he identified the road kill some years back.

What a fucking reunion! The engine stalled a couple of times, and when it started, all I could think of was sweet Candy on my tongue, until dispatch came in announcing a shooting that had just taken place at Phillips Arena. It didn't take too long for me to put two and two together, and I knew that it had something to do with Xavier. I headed straight there anticipating seeing Bobby's dead corpse with a confirmed look of shock on his face. But when I got there, it was more than I wished for.

I called Candy and told her not to wait up; I had a homicide on my hands.

IF I . . .

"I'm here at Philips Arena where just twenty-minutes ago a horrendous shooting took place, causing two fatalities and multiple injuries, including Atlanta's own recording artist Vgo D'artiste, who sustained a single gunshot wound to the abdomen area. There's no word on his condition right now, but the shooter, whose identity hasn't been released just yet, was gunned down by police officers moments after the shooting took place. At this time, we don't know the shooter's motive, but we're receiving information right now as I'm reporting the story live to you.

"Okay, word just got in that the shooter's name was Xavier Cooper; a former employee of Good Game Records, and known criminal. Standing here next to me is the vice president of the label, Bobby Williams.

"Mr. Williams, why did the shooter commit such a heinous act? And who was his intended target?"

"At this moment I can't comment on Xavier's motive, but he was experiencing a high-frequency of stress, and I approved his leave of absence this morning. He was not expected to be here tonight."

"Did you have a personal relationship with him?"

"I have a relationship with all of my employees to a certain extent; and as a company, we con-

194

sider ourselves to be a family. It's unfortunate what happened tonight, and we will be carefully reviewing backgrounds extensively for future employees. I'm pretty sure Vgo D'artiste was not the intended target, and we're praying that he pulls through. Also, we send our love to the Cooper family. We mourn their loss, and with the exception of that loss, we will pay the funeral expenses for the departed, as well as the doctor fees for the injured. I'm sorry, but I have to go."

"There you have it, ladies and gentlemen; there will be more coverage at eleven o'clock tonight; and once again, this is Angela Carpenter, back to you, Tom."

When I left the interview I had two things on my mind: Vgo D'artiste and Lonnie's condition. The only difference was that I wanted one alive and the other dead. When I got to the hospital Vgo was in emergency surgery, and after a rigid and very uncomfortable wait, we received good news that he would make a stable recovery. But if the bullet had been just a quarter-inch to the left of his kidney, he wouldn't have made it. Finding that out was a relief to us all; and after being hounded by the press and dealing with fans trying to see him in his torn and lacerated state, I begged Jesus to turn my water into wine.

James stayed at the hospital and I went home. When I got there, Stacy held me tight and I didn't want her to let go. I couldn't help but remember String's face before the shooting, but it bothered me even more seeing him get shot to death. I didn't get to hear his last words. If only he could have told me that Lonnie was dead!

"I watched them, baby. I watched them shoot the shit out of String.

He just snapped. He was trying to kill me! When I saw him, Vgo D'artiste was in the middle of his performance. I walked toward him back-stage, and he just started shooting. Vgo was hit first, and I hid behind a speaker with one of the models; then she tried to run. All I remember was her getting up and falling back down with a hole in her neck, and blood everywhere. I could hear her gurgle blood, and fight through what little time and pain God allowed her to enjoy before he brought her home. I thought I was next until I heard a bunch of yelling and resistance, followed by multiple shots. I peeked around the speaker and saw the police take him down. All I could think of was you and the baby. Don't let go, Stacy"

"I'll never leave you, Bobby. I love you."

"I'm tired, baby."

"Me too; let's go upstairs."

My phone was blowing up until I turned it off. I just needed to be held like a toddler who relies on his mother to protect him.

I was fucked up and didn't know where to go or who to talk to. I felt trapped in a bubble of lies and deceit. Sleep became just as helpful as alcohol, because I didn't have to worry while under the influence of both.

That night set the tone for my unforgettable downfall, but I guess that's why I'm writing this story, so that maybe my mistake won't be repeated. I didn't bother attending String's funeral because I was still a little shaken, and a bit curious to why he tried to kill me. So I sent my regards and kept it movin'!

A year and a half later . . .

The first two years after the shooting at the arena was hard on James and his personal life, but he got over Jennifer completely. He was back to the CEO that I knew he could be. Within the first year, Vgo D'artiste recuperated with a vengeance and an obvious bet to collect from me, once he received that platinum plaque.

The news of his shooting boosted record sales and the streets highly anticipated his next release. And with some of the hottest producers eager to work with him, Vgo D'artiste was definitely being pre-approved for a double-platinum selling record, and "My Kinda Girl' climbed to the top of the charts, which helped skyrocket Sydne's record sales as well. Shit, if he wasn't the hottest rapper out, then Popeye was most definitely a punk! We were determined to take over the game and were focused more than ever with higher standards, goals, and expectations for the company as a whole.

Even though money was never an issue with me, happiness in my life always had its ups and downs. I guess the Lord permitted me a little of it so that I'd take advantage of it with my family. I decided to move because we needed a bigger place. I needed a pool, and Bobby Jr. needed a bigger room for his toys and shit. It seemed like we were as high as we could get financially; and I mean *so high,* we had to wear earplugs when we spent our money.

We announced live on the morning show the official date for Vgo D'artiste's new album release. Thousands of dollars in advertising paid off when James showed me the demographic reviews, Internet blogs, and articles about the project titled "Forks and Knives". I was proud to admit that we were the kings of the south and Good Game Records was opening doors for the underdogs.

Atlanta's music scene was like the West, when N.W.A. was representing, or the East, when Wu-Tang Clan was getting that dollar-dollar bill. Vgo D'artiste's album release party was like the presidential inauguration, except that in this case, our presence was appreciated. I couldn't count how many attractive women were in the club and Stacy was on me like shit on a pamper, but it's okay for a brotha to look at the merchandise as long as he don't touch, right?

The party was an official red carpet affair, with limousines pulling up, and celebrities coming to pop bottles with the hottest rappers on the scene. The result of our hard work showed on this spectacular night, and those involved knew that it wasn't an easy task to complete.

Everyone that grinded with us to help establish our empire deserved to be commended for his or her persistence. Vgo D'artiste, James, and I were the men of the hour, and Vgo D'artiste received the most praise, considering he almost lost his life a year back to help us get where we were. But if it weren't for Sydne holding it down for a while, we could have lost everything.

It was beautiful! James and I were inseparable that night, and by our demeanor, you would have thought that we were the happiest music executives alive. Shit, to be honest, I even bought into it. Throughout the night, there were plenty of performances and announcements. It gave our label an opportunity to display the musical team that we assembled over the years.

I turned to James and said, "We're back, my nigga, just you and I." I hugged him, not knowing if it was the champagne or what, but at that time, considering the shit that we'd been through, it was necessary to identify the fact that even in the end, we could at least count on each other. It's like Jennifer never existed; it was taboo to even speak her name, and I guess that's what it took for James to move on.

James refilled my glass, wrapping his arm around me to speak. "I just wanna thank you for having my back, dog; you always have, even when you were locked up. I owe you more than you can even imagine, but . . . Enough of this emotional shit; we run Atlanta, so let's enjoy ourselves."

He raised his hand high, dressed in his True Religion jeans and blazer, with Gucci shades, looking like a made man. I picked up a champagne bottle to refill Stacy's glass to toast to our success, but it was empty, so I excused myself to head to the bar. On my way to get the drinks, people were stopping me to speak and handing me demos, so it took some time for me to get there. And when I did, I decided to stay for a shot.

In the process of getting the bartenders attention, I heard a familiar voice—the voice of a dead man! "Long time, old friend."

I turned around with a cold feeling down my spine and an instinct to take the shot quickly, because it was probably gonna be my last. I was speechless for the first time in my life as Lonnie Biggs continued to speak, "You don't look too happy to see me. Well, I wouldn't be either if I were looking death in the eyes. Your days are numbered, mothafucka! Did you like the surprise that I sent you, Bobby?"

I didn't know what kind of games he was playing.

"What surprise?"

"I would advise you to check your mail more often, Bobby. They didn't teach you how to read in prison?"

He raised his glass and toasted me without my permission and said, "This is to Millertime and Xavier; their blood didn't spill in vain."

He took his shot and hopped off the stool, bumping my shoulder as he walked past me. *"Where has he been for the past year and a half?"* He looked at me with a smirk, and I couldn't believe I was confronted by a man who supposed to be entertaining the devil. I grabbed my bottle and stormed through the dancing crowd to find Stacy, and when I did, I grabbed her shoulder and spoke as clear as I have ever spoken before.

"Listen to me, baby, and listen to me carefully. A year and half ago, right around the time that String was killed, did you ever receive some mail for me that you may have overlooked because I was gone or something? Because if you did, please tell me that you know where it is."

She recognized the seriousness of this matter and said, "Baby, you're squeezing me!"

"Stacy, just answer the question."

"Yes, baby, it's in the garage somewhere. I'll find it. I never throw away anything unless I talk to you first, so it has to be at the house. I'm sorry, are you okay?"

I kissed her on the forehead and hugged her before apologizing.

I poured Stacy a glass of champagne from the bottle that I got from the bar and asked her about James. She told me that he'd headed to the office for an important phone call, so I headed back there to see what was up. When I opened the door, I immediately knew something was wrong when I saw him. He was staring at the phone in his right hand, with his left hand covering his mouth. He didn't even look this hurt at my sister's funeral.

"Hey, man, what's wrong?"

"Bobby . . . Bob-by," he tried to talk, but it seemed like what he'd just heard devastated him so much, that his eight-ounce educated brain still couldn't register the news that was delivered. Unable to speak, James put his head down and I began to see drool pour out of his mouth. His fist started to clench, and the veins in his neck and temple started to protrude. I ran over to grab his shoulder and push him back to view his face, when he voluntarily threw himself in an upward position.

What I witnessed was true emotion. His eyes were wide open and mouth as well, but there was no breathing or sound to be heard. And all of a sudden like an embarrassed child, he inhaled quickly before letting everything out, then he began to cry, and I had no idea why until minutes later when he let me into his world of hardship.

"Jennifer is dead, my nigga."

"What?" I said.

"Her mother just called me and said she's been with her in Memphis since she left me; and her health took a serious turn for the worse, just last year. She's been in the hospital for a week and it was nothing that they could do. Her body was just tired, man.

"Two fucking years she has been gone from me, and two of those years it took for me to get over her. I mean, the last time I saw her was the day Bobby Jr. was born, and now I hear that she's dead! Feelings that I thought I'd buried are beginning to resurface, man. She was everything to me."

I just stood there, just as hurt to hear the news as he was, and there I was, unable to physically show my reaction to the news of her death, so I tried to conceal it out of discretion. I was prohibited to have even the slightest connection or bond with Jennifer the way that James did, but since I did, it made my grieving a little more difficult than the average friend.

Internally I was broken and started to have trouble breathing. I combined my emotions, perpetrating my condolences to make it appear to be as if I were there with James during his hard times. Our devastation was just as equal. I was affected deeply and even though I tried, I just couldn't conceal it. Her death took me for a loop when I heard how she'd suffered, and it didn't add up until James confessed shortly after he gathered himself.

He stared at me slowly, blinking once and then twice, before letting it all go, "Bobby, what I'm about to tell you is something that I've kept to myself, and it has overwhelmed me with seclusion, misplacing my ability to choose what is and what is not. I can only play the fly on a wall in a world of good fortune, and a life promised to those with spiritual abundance. Here I am, left in a hole with nowhere else to look but up, while marking my own calendar in hopes to cherish another day.

"In the beginning of my whirlwind of melancholy I was troubled, but love and I overcame my fear, adapted quickly to the reality of spending the rest of my life with Jennifer, and didn't have any disputes whatsoever. I learned to accept my path that has been chosen for me.

"She changed me in many ways and I'm not sure if I would even be here, and I know I wouldn't feel the way that I do if it wasn't for her. The reason behind my confession to you concerning her death is that deep down in my heart, I loved her so much, that without her, I knew it would be hard for me to live; and I prayed to God on many occasions to die before her, when the time came. This shit is hard to deal with, but I've got to get it out."

I didn't know where he was going with this, and when he was talking, it seemed like he was confessing to himself rather than me, but I encouraged him to continue.

"James, I'm here for you, man. Just let it go."

"Jennifer and I made a decision years ago when we planted our seed as a couple in the beginning. Not exactly because we thought it was faith, or that we identified ourselves as soul mates, Bobby, but I decided to forgive, forget, and make it work with her after she contracted me with the AIDS virus. I couldn't deal with the possible regret in the back of my mind in regards to infecting others, and fell in love with her in the process, until I realized that she was my soul mate—and now she's gone. This shit is real, Bobby! And I'm dying slow, my nigga!"

My knees got weak, so I took a seat to comprehend what I'd just heard. I would have liked to believe that it was a possibility I wasn't infected with the virus, but Jennifer and I were having unprotected sex on a regular basis. I began to get sick, and even considered joining in with James and crying myself. I felt James's pain, but I also had questions of my own that were racing through my head—like how long do I have to live—and did I infect my family? We just sat there in deep thought about the secret he had just revealed, but it didn't encourage me in any way to share my own.

"So what are you gonna do about the funeral?"

"I told Jennifer's mother that I would pay for everything. She died yesterday evening, so the funeral will be Saturday. Are you going?"

"Yeah, homie, I'll be there."

"Thanks, Bobby. I need all the support that I can get right now. I never told you because I didn't want you to look at me different, ya know?"

"I just wish you would have, so we could have maybe prevented some things that occurred, ya know?"

I left the office with my bottle in hand to find another place to isolate myself. I preferred to be home, so I text messaged Stacy to let her know that I was leaving. When I got home, I took a hot and steamy shower before I attempted to drink my sorrows away. I found myself on the floor and drunk as hell, thinking about my life and what is yet to come from it. I never thought that I would ever be a victim of such a massive and deadly epidemic. Only hookers, hoes, and homos catch that shit. At least that's what I thought. Jennifer was educated, fine, and she looked healthy. I would've never known, but unfortunately it took me to increase the statistic to realize that any one of us could be infected, or get infected. Condoms save lives, and not just take the sensational feeling away.

About an hour and a half after I got home, Stacy picked me up from the floor and tried to help me to bed, but I felt contaminated, so I settled for the couch. And besides, being alone was all I could ask for at that point. That cycle continued until Saturday.

The Funeral . . .

We arrived in Memphis just hours before the funeral. James mentioned a couple of stories about Jennifer's immediate family that he didn't agree with, and only wanted to attend the funeral to pay his respects to his lost love, before continuing with his own life. And I didn't know where to start with my own at that point in time.

Destroying your own life is a hard issue to deal with and can be fixed eventually; and if not, then it's your life that you fucked up. But being responsible for someone else's is a situation that you'd rather not experience, especially if it's your future wife and son. I haven't been the best friend, lover or father, and I guess this was karma's way of telling me that everything has a consequence, even attraction.

Sitting in my room gave me time to think, but I found myself forming an alliance with the mini bar. It's hard accepting the fact that you're fucked up and the end result can't be bought or paid off. It's a hard thing to swallow and a tough situation to overlook. I let greed and lack of integrity get the best of me, and it was too late to forget or even ask for forgiveness. The best thing to do was keep it hidden for as long as I could. Deep down I am really a good nigga, but I had a sweet tooth for temptation, and I lost myself in the process.

We arrived at Collierville Funeral Home at eleven in the morning. I've been to too many already, but I guess there was always room for one more. Jennifer's arrangement was beautiful, considering the circumstances, but I could tell that we weren't going to stay too long. On our way out, Jennifer's mother approached James to give him some much-needed information.

"Hello, James. I wanna thank you for everything that you have done for Jennifer and the expenses for the funeral. If there is anything that I can do personally, please let me know."

She hugged James before he spoke, "No, Ms. Nelson, if there is anything that I can do for *you,* just let *me* know. A mother should never experience a child's death before her own. I've grieved as a lover and a friend, but I could never be compared to a parent's loss. I loved her and will always miss her."

They hugged and Jennifer's mother continued, "You know, my daughter loved you very much and despite our differences, James, I've always respected your commitment to Jennifer.

"She never told me why she left you, and I guess nobody will ever know now, but whatever it was, she just couldn't deal with it, and her love for you wouldn't allow her to hurt you more than she has already. She was battling a few demons and whatever regrets it was that she held close to her dear heart, just picked and picked at her sweet soul. These past few years have been hard on us all, but a blessing did come out of it. James, I have someone for you to meet."

Jennifer's mother signaled a little girl over to join their company, and then Ms. Nelson continued, "My granddaughter has been waiting to hear her father's voice for three years; isn't she pretty? She has your eyes."

James got on his knees with an awkward look of amazement on his face. I was really happy, and me being the closest person to James besides Jennifer, I knew how much it meant to him now that she was deceased.

The youth resurrects the misfortune in us all, and the responsibility of parenthood would nearly revive my old friend.

Everyone crowded around to enjoy this unforgettable attachment. The little girl just stood there, eager to initiate her companionship but still quite nervous, in this highly-anticipated confrontation.

James began to speak, "Hey, pretty lady, I like your dress. I didn't think something so beautiful could be created by me. I'm glad to be your father, and we've got much catching up to do. Can I have a hug?"

She ran to him and they embraced.

James looked up to Ms. Nelson and asked, "Can she speak well?"

"Can she! She's a smart and articulate little thing."

James separated himself before speaking to the girl and asked, "So, what's your name?"

The shy girl bit her pinky finger then rubbed her eye as if it was irritated before smiling and cheerfully said, "BOBBY."

James looked at me with rapid suspicion that only we could catch wind of, and while everyone literally sensed a good vibe turning sour by the way James was reacting, nobody knew what the outcome was about to escalate to—but me.

"Why the hell is my daughter named after you? Bobby, you backstabbing son of a bitch! Not again . . . This can't be happening."

I think I instantly caught a fever the minute I heard my name being called, and what did he mean by saying "not again"? My body was so hot, I literally had to bend over and rest my hands on my knees. It was over, and the truth could no longer be avoided.

"Hey, man, let's not jump to conclusions. I don't have a clue what you're talking about right now." My time was up and the firing squad was locked and loaded!

When I woke up that morning, I never thought my day would get even worse until James got up.

At the funeral he suddenly headed toward me, saying, "Yeah, it all makes sense to me now, and I understand everything perfectly clear. You and Jennifer were fucking around behind my back the whole fucking time; but how long? Long enough for her to conceive your child, right?

"I guess she couldn't live with the fact that she was cheating on me with my best friend. Is that why she left, so you and I could preserve our friendship? She left me because of *you*. All the women in the world and you had to run mine away, *you bastard!*"

"I don't know why she left, man. You're assuming all the wrong things, I swear," I pleaded but I knew it was over.

"But she left you with something that you can never return with a receipt, and I hope it kills you quicker that I, BITCH!"

James hit me in the face and before I could react, I was already lying between a row of pews. Nobody could restrain him as he picked me up by my shirt and hit me again. Enabled by my embarrassment, I became weak; a worthless piece of shit who pissed away a secure future, and not to mention, the father of an unwanted daughter. When the fight broke out, it was confirmed that my secret was out of the bag and my friendship with James was incapable of patching.

Everybody yelled, including the pastor, "Stop, guys, please—before somebody gets hurt. There are children present, please stop."

There was only so much that I could take and by this time, James was man handling me all the way to the front and near the podium. He swung and I ducked, grabbing him by his neck. We spun each other in circles in the most careless and frustrating rage. The only difference between our rages was it was exceptional for James, considering that I chased away what small happiness he had in his life. My anger, on the other hand, was displayed merely out of embarrassment that I was finally caught.

We were acting like fools until I pushed as hard as I could, not realizing Jennifer's casket was behind him. My force threw him into the casket knocking it over and revealing the content, reminding us all why we were there in the first place. Everybody screamed, sighed and cried as they witnessed this unbelievable incident take place before their eyes.

"Stop it now!! Oh my God, someone help him up . . . Lord Jesus," a voice said from behind me. I just stood there with intentions to leave immediately, but I couldn't help but observe as I noticed Jennifer's lifeless body hanging halfway out of the casket; her long hair covering her face and her hand went free from its original position at the viewing.

James was tangled between the casket and the flowers having no control of his fall. Everybody screamed and when James tried to get himself together, he turned to his left and was face-to-face with her. I watched his anger change dramatically into the loving husband that he yearned to be; a lion protecting his territory and allowing no one to disrupt his moment. His hands hesitated to touch her and when he did, he looked up to the ceiling and closed his eyes before placing his head on hers saying, "Baby, I'm sorry. I hated you for leaving me alone the way you did. I took your presence for granted at times, but it's important to me that you're free. I want you to wait for me, baby."

He held her while he wept until a couple of men approached him to reorganize the setting, and to prepare Jennifer's burial. I managed to make my exit without anymore words being said, and on my way out I kept hearing James say, "I can't forgive you, Bobby, big mistakes or the small ones. I can't forgive and never will. I can never overlook the small ones, Bobby."

As soon as I got back to the room, I packed my shit and got the fuck out of Memphis, and that was the least of my problems!

THE LAST LAUGH

I prayed to God that my plane would crash on the way back to Atlanta, because my life as I knew it was over. I worked hard to build a company that I couldn't legally prove in court that I partially owned, so I was no longer employed. James found out that I was sleeping with his fiancée, so I no longer had a friend. I've used those closest to me for personal gain in my selfish schemes to stay on top, separating my self- respect from my conscious, and I could no longer sleep peaceful.

My health was permanently stained, infecting my family as well, giving me no reason to look forward to a loving future, and not to mention, Lonnie Biggs.

I was tired and didn't have the answers or the energy for my next move. I caught a cab home from the airport and managed to squeeze in a liquor store run on my way. I guess the Lord was feeling my pain because it was beginning to drizzle. We were supposed to move a month after the funeral but, since James owned my home, I thought it would be a good idea to leave as soon as possible, because it was only a matter of time before he kicked me out.

Why couldn't everything just stay cool? I was devastated and didn't know who to call or who to run to about my problems. I know what I did was shady, and the more I thought about the feelings and lives that I put at risk, I realized that every decision a person makes affects the people they love.

In the midst of all my personal issues, Stacy came through with some good news. "Hey, baby, I just closed on a four bedroom, three bathroom house in Mount Vernon, and I'm glad because we needed to step-up anyway."

"That's great, babe," I said with as little enthusiasm as possible.

"I'd think you'd be a little happier than that, Bobby. This is the house that we wanted, remember? Are you okay?"

"Yeah, I've got a lot of crap on my mind that's all, but I'm happy."

I wanted to believe that everything was going to be fine. Stacy was so happy and energetic about getting the house, and all the great blessings that we've recently received, so I just sat there unable and unwilling to interfere with her special moment.

On her way out with Bobby Jr. she backed up and said, "Oh, and, baby, I found that package that you asked me about. When I was cleaning, I just put it up and forgot about it, baby. I'm so sorry. I'm on my way out to sign some paperwork and pick up some things for Bobby Jr. You look tired, honey, do you need anything while I'm out?"

"No, baby, I'm just a little under the weather. I'll let this Hennessy help me sweat it out."

I tried to keep my pain buried as deep as possible. I just needed a few minutes to get my mind right. I knew Stacy like the back of my hand, and as wired as she was acting, I was already hip to the notion that she wanted some loving. But where I was mentally, I couldn't get in the mood if I wanted to. I stared at the television wishing that I could change the channel in my life, and if I could, knowing how bad my luck has been lately, the fucking batteries would have been dead by the time I got the remote anyway!

When she got to the door she asked, "How was the funeral?"

"Let's just say it changed my outlook on things, life in particular."

Stacy left and I locked the door behind her. I couldn't wait to open my two-year-old mail, courtesy of Mr. Biggs. I hesitated for a while, and during that hesitation, I drifted into a lonely world of defeat and heartache. I felt like Mike Tyson when he refused to leave his stool in the sixth round against McBride, or a kidnapped journalist in Pakistan who has no idea what lies in his future, or even James Brown when he took his last breath of life, leaving the only world where he was known as "King."

I started to drink and reflect on the past, and I guess I got what I asked for when I said that I wished I had what James and Jennifer had, when I began to envy their happiness at the restaurant. I've been horribly dishonest and disloyal to my loved ones who had listened, supported, and given me chances, and since it's all over, who else can I run to other than Stacy? No one; she was all I had until my whole world dissolved before me, piece by piece, but nothing was more heartbreaking than the phone call that I received from Stacy two hours after she left.

When I answered I was already down and out and didn't think things could get worse.

"Hello!"

"Tell me it isn't true, Bobby."

"Hello!"

"Bobby, you fucking hear me! I can't believe you. James told me everything that you've been doing, you fucking snake. You and Jennifer had a baby together? Is that why she left? I can't fucking stand you. I just got off the phone with James and he told me everything about you two, and added that there was more that I needed to know, but he didn't want to spoil some surprise that you had for me! What is it? And you better be honest."

"Babe, just come back home and we'll talk about it," I said, but she wasn't having it at all. I guess there is a flipside to every coin, and even though dealing with the good was ever so exciting, dealing with the bad was also part of the deal that I made with the devil.

"No, Bobby, I can't even look at you right now. I don't think I'm going to be able to get over this just overnight. I love you, but this hurts!"

"Listen, I know I fucked up and yes, we got involved, but I love you though. I'm with you!" I said, and even though it makes sense to us men when it's said, a real woman would never by that line, and that's exactly what she was.

"So let me get this straight; you've been fucking our child's godmother, who was also James's fiancée? If that bitch wasn't dead, I swear I'd kill her ass. And you . . . Ooh—you know what, Bobby, just tell me everything so I can end this conversation."

In the middle of preparing for my confession that was sure to end my world, I put the phone on speaker. I was unable to control my sense of touch and became numb with guilt.

"I know you hear me, nigga, so you don't have anything to say? Everything you touch turns to shit. I'm so pissed off. I wasn't good enough for you, you had to go fuck somebody else, and Jennifer at that? I was always there for you and believed you when you told me that you were ready. You don't owe me any excuses, Bobby. All I want is to hear the truth from your mouth. Tell me what James couldn't tell me."

I wasn't prepared to play the cards that were in front of me, and since I was the dealer, it hurt me deep to deliver the terrible news to those that I loved the most. I guess I wasn't the man that I thought I was, because it was too much pressure to handle, and hurting my baby the way that I did and being forced to admit to it, was not only hard to follow through, but it was difficult to comprehend the results of my selfish actions. I've handed down more than my attractive genes to my loving son, who is already cursed by my tainted name. It's situations like these that make you wanna close your eyes and never wake up.

All she wanted was to hear the rest of what James failed to finish, so I closed my eyes and took a deep breath before I spoke, "Stacy, I never meant to hurt you, and I do love you, very much so, but at that time I was controlled by attraction and lost in lust. It was only you two, I swear. I know I fucked up and—"

Stacy cut me off with a high and intolerable tone. I could tell she had been crying and she was really hurt, as her objections took over the conversation. "Bobby shut up, just shut up. None of it is true so just tell me already. You owe me at least that don't you think?"

Fuck it! I man'd up and told her.

"Okay, Stacy, okay. I never expected to— damn, baby—okay, you know about me and Jennifer, but what you don't know and what I found out last week was that . . ., baby, I love you—shit—Jennifer had HIV, and it's a strong chance of you and Bobby being infected too!"

One of my feet were already in the grave and the other was standing on a banana peel, and when I confessed, I might as well have taken my last breath because it took all of me to tell her that tomorrow definitely wasn't promised to her, because of a careless mistake created by the man who was supposed to protect them. There was a brief pause and it was as dead as my future, until I heard Stacy's cracked voice, "OH-MY-GOD, OH MY GOD, BOBBY! HOW COULD YOU! M-M-M-My, God."

Stacy couldn't handle it. Her life was going so well and she always talked about the future with grandkids, and was already deciding what our son should be when he grew up, and I took that from her: her dreams, memories, and her reason to ever smile again. Stacy was all I had, and giving her that news closed the window for reconciliation.

"How could you, Bobby? I gave you everything I had and I just don't have anymore to give. . . ."

She ended the call, and when I looked at my phone to see if she was still there, all I saw was my son's picture on my screensaver. I was furious and threw my phone at the wall, watching it shatter instantly, and just like my iPhone, I was also in pieces. I trashed my house and everything that I could get my hands on until I sat down.

I started to hyperventilate and needed to catch my breath, and when I did, I looked down at the table in front of me. All that I have worked hard for and have loved over the past five years has been reduced to a mysterious old package that concealed a piece of history that changed my life forever.

I ripped it open to find a journal, and found myself shocked to notice my sister's handwriting. By this time it was raining heavily and the skies were thundering with anger. Most of the pages were marked with black ink, making the majority of the pages unreadable, but the last few pages were untouched and upon reading them, they started to get very interesting.

Today was a great day for me and I would like to thank God for opening my heart and finally giving me the opportunity to identify my true love. But love can be tricky sometimes, and I've dealt with a lot of dudes who told me that they loved me and wanted to take care of me just so they could get some ass, and it's funny . . . because in some instances, I allowed myself to fall for a couple of them; not because I was dumb, but shit, I was bored, and a bitch needed some dick!

But it's not like that with these two guys. I found the best of both worlds: a street nigga and a corporate brotha. I feel like I've discovered a double-sided coin, but with different value on each side. I've known Millertime forever and he's my heart. We've been there for each other, even when our backs were sore from being against that wall so long. I learned a lot from him and visa versa, and even though

I stopped working for him, we remained friends and our relationship escalated into something that I never imagined possible. But in the process of playing tug of war with his ass, I met and fell hard for James. OH, he is just the shit.

He's got his priorities straight and I know he'll be big one day!! I took him for a square when I first met him, but after the life that I lived, I needed a new perspective and he was a good start. He was patient. He listened and treated me with respect. It wasn't too long before we were dating and also getting serious. I fell in love with two men, but I'm madly in love with one.

I talked to my mother about aborting James's child, and she gave me some good advice after our altercation when she heard me talking to Millertime about it. She thought James appeared to be sneaky, but had fewer good things to say about him in comparison to Millertime, even though she disagreed with his lifestyle. My brother is so overprotective but he knows me better than anybody, I mean we are twins and think just alike with our selfish assess! I need to see him so he can help me make a decision, because I can't continue to live two lives and lose out on something good.

Now that I'm sitting here writing this letter, comparisons between them are matching and

I can't deny my intentions to make him happy, make him love me, make him call my name as I will call his. I love him. I love everything about him, from his walk to how his name rolls off my tongue: MILL-ER-TIME.

We will always be together and I've never thought about moving on without him. I guess James is just my go-to guy, but as long as my boo allows me to love him, I will forever. I would rather be with him in his world than alone in mine. Tonight, after I see my brother, I'm gonna do James the favor of letting him go. He's going to take it hard, because I know he loves me, but it has to be done so I can move on.

I dropped the journal and couldn't believe what I'd just read.

Flashbacks of incidents unraveled as far as her aborting James's baby, and now I know what he meant at the funeral when he said, "Not again." And the night before Pamela's murder also gave clues that I didn't catch as well.

I knew when I met her at the Sundial that she was bothered about something serious, because I'd never seen her so undetermined. And when she left, after our conversation was interrupted by her phone call, she looked relieved, as though she was encouraged to confront the problem herself, which initiated our get together in the first place. But the truth about what really happened and who was really responsible for his son's murder was the collateral that Lonnie Biggs had, and held until the perfect time to assist my rage.

I've been getting played since day one, and even though I just wanted to lie down and wake up to my perfect world again, it was unlikely. Now it was time to get my hands dirty and close the chapter to this catastrophic story.

The journal was the bridge that connected everything that I finally needed to know, and all I knew was what James told me, until I did something that I never took time to do on my own: think outside the box; when it hit me. Who else but a heartbroken man, unable to control his emotions over the women he loved, considered death an option? Who else was clever enough to separate himself from trouble once he got what he wanted out of a deal? Who else would take to my sister's beliefs in regards to love being nothing but two people feeling sorry for each other, and adopt it to himself? Who else would never want me to socialize with the only man that had the knowledge to reveal his twisted veracity and spontaneous favors, spawned from guilt that he used, to keep me blind until now?

I sat back and thought about Millertime's last words, and I will never forget them.

"Change, Change, Change."

I was dead wrong with what I thought I heard him say.

What he was telling me before I blew his head off was, "*James, James, James,*" making me responsible for another man's life. Not the life of the man who murdered my sister in cold blood, but the man that was known to her as her true love. James felt betrayed once he found out that Pamela was leaving him for an ex-pimp, and stabbed her in a jealous rage in the middle of a heated altercation. He already took it hard after finding out about the abortion and took her back, but couldn't handle losing her over Millertime; his ex-partner's pimp of a son.

After covering up the murder, he was aware that Millertime was the only man that could put him behind bars, so he manipulated me, Pamela's closest friend and sibling, to tie his loose ends for him. I guess he really did owe me more than I could ever imagine, and had made a commitment to himself, feeling obligated to take care of me, out of guilt for taking my other half from me. I finally knew why he didn't act out as much as I expected him to at her funeral!

Finding out the truth about my sister's murder woke up the killa in me, and I found myself preparing to leave my house to pay James an unexpected visit. I remember mentioning that James could never betray me the way I did him, and I couldn't stand to see him in any pain. I considered him my brother and embraced him endearingly, only to find out in the end, that the whole time he was buying my friendship in exchange for my ignorance to the eye-popping fact that it was because of him that I buried my sister.

Now I understand the real cause behind his generosity, and I couldn't identify with my patience as I took time to relive Pamela's murder. Step by step, I felt her getting stabbed repeatedly, and all I could see was James on top of her with his knife, penetrating her with sharp steel with no intentions of her enjoying any minute of it. I saw her fighting for her life, her hands waving to prevent facial wounds until she couldn't take anymore. Her body gives up, allowing him to proceed without struggle, and while his anger motivates him to continue, Pamela's life turns into a corpse. Her eyes tell the story of her scandal, and it's like I was there with her, but unable to interfere with the fate that she was given.

Everybody that I dealt with in the past five years has been poison in my life. James came into my life and corrupted me, Jennifer came into my life and tempted me, Stacy came into my life and loved me, and I'm yet to know Lonnie Biggs's plans on finishing what I started.

My reaction to the flashback caused me to drop my bottle and I followed shortly, finding myself on my knees. I was so irate, my violent behavior and domestic tantrums sobered me, and I was ready to play in the final segment of a reality series that had no more lifelines. I ran upstairs and laced my ankles with my nigga chasers; and two things on my mind: a chance to repent and the honor to spill James's blood.

Unlike my incident with Millertime, I didn't plan on shooting him, but decided to take my gun just in case, but it wasn't there. Stacy always complained about it being around the house since Bobby Jr. was into things, and I guess she finally got rid of it.

I wanted James to feel the same pain that Pamela did, so I headed to the kitchen to grab the sharpest knife that I could find. I called James from the house phone but it kept going to voice mail, giving me the answer that I inquired to know. I hoped his conversation was a good one, because I was sure it would be his last.

When I got into my car, something was awkward, but I disregarded it because of my hunger to put a nigga under. I positioned my seat, turned the ignition, put the shift in drive, and moved out. It's crazy how a man's life can diminish right before his own eyes, but when an outsider takes a glance in those very same eyes, he responds with a careless expression, simply unaware of his problems, nor understands the reality that he's forced to wake up to.

As I obeyed the traffic laws, calm, collected and on my way to subtract the population by one, I cried while realizing whose life I was out for. I made a turn on his street, reducing my speed to ten miles an hour before cutting my lights off and parking my car. The thrill was gone and it was time to move on. I was ready to free myself from his spell. Before I exited my car, I looked into my rearview mirror and didn't recognize the man in it. Bobby Williams no longer existed; he was a victim, a cast away, and a convict.

I snuck around to the back of his condo and his sliding door was unlocked. I took a deep breath and walked in. Marvin Gaye and Tammy Terrell were playing and all of the lights were on downstairs. He wasn't in the kitchen or living room, so I headed upstairs with my knife in hand to greet him as an enemy and not a friend.

Each step meant I was closer to my goal. I made it to the top and I felt the wall in search for a light switch, when my phone rang. It startled me and in the process of me silencing it, I stumbled over an object on the floor. I caught myself and hit the switch, hoping I didn't blow my cover when I discovered the object that I tripped over; it was James, lying dead on the floor with two holes in the back of the head, with his eyes open and holding his cordless phone.

I dropped my knife and ran downstairs, pacing until I got it together, but my phone kept fucking ringing, so I answered it and screamed, "WHAT?"

"Payback's a bitch, ain't it, Bobby?"

"Who is this?"

"A better friend to you than that piece of shit lying on that floor in there; at least I hate you enough to tell you that you're fucked!"

"Lonnie, I swear on my mother's grave, you're fucking dead, you hear me? DEAD!"

As soon as Lonnie Biggs hung up, the police rushed in yelling at the top of their lungs, and when I heard, "Get on the floor now!" I knew I had underestimated him. I complied and they handcuffed me before sitting me down. They didn't have shit on me, though. James had gunshot wounds and I had a knife. I remained calm on the couch with a smirk, just waiting to talk to my five-hundred-dollar-an-hour lawyer and until then, I was mute. What were they gonna do?

All of that confidence went sour when Lonnie Biggs walked in with another officer, and my gun, that I thought Stacy had gotten rid of, in a plastic evidence bag.

"I found this weapon underneath the seat of the suspect's vehicle. Check it for prints, Detective."

When I saw him, I already knew what time it was; I was witnessing a real master plan, playing into the hands of my opponent, right before my eyes. I was being framed and couldn't do anything about it. It was Lonnie Biggs who stole my gun from the house, used it to kill James, and put it in my car right before I drove over here. The only person who drove my car was me, and I should have known something was up when I had to readjust my seat. I was done!

I sat on the couch with my hands cuffed behind my back and nervous to the tenth power, and since I was going down, I figured I'd get to thinking ahead and I needed to know who in this world loved me enough, after what I did, to support me this time. I had ten fingers and ten toes, and couldn't count one who still loved me! When I put my head down, tears began to stain my cross trainers.

Lonnie Biggs approached me and said, "Look at me, mothafucka; look at me!"

I looked up and he continued as he whispered, "You thought you couldn't be touched, little nigga. I played you like the bitch that you are, and it still ain't over, Bobby."

He hit me in my face before handing me over to be transferred to the station. When I was escorted outside by Lonnie Biggs he was on the phone.

"Yeah, return the message, deputy, and tell him I'm calling in that favor; he'll know what I'm talking about. Yes, that's correct, Bobby Williams."

Stacy was in front to witness the aftermath as well as the whole fucking neighborhood. The news of James's murder made headlines everywhere and my case was televised. I was labeled as the greedy apprentice who killed his friend/partner for all of the power, and the media had a field day with it.

The evidence against me was overwhelming and numerous witnesses stepped up, testifying that my car was seen at the residence before, during, and after the murder took place. Considering my prints were on the gun and it actually being the murder weapon, on top of me calling him from my phone before the murder, it made my defense weak and it wasn't looking good for me. It was seriously leaning toward a guilty conviction, and spending the rest of my natural young life in prison was something that I should have been considering at that point.

My lawyer advised me to cop a temporary insanity plea, and it worked. He focused on my inexperience in the corporate surroundings, pointing out the stressful area of responsibility that I was forced to deal with during James's absence from the company during his rehabilitation, that later led to infidelity with his significant other, and finding out about the Aids, caused a devastating affliction, later instigating a production for retaliation that I obviously was unable to control. I agreed and was sentenced to twenty years to life with the possibility of parole.

Stacy didn't come to court during any of the arraignments, and it hurt me most to walk out of the courtroom without seeing my son after my conviction. When the judge banged that gavel, I remember thinking, *Damn, I should have followed my instincts when I got into my car,* but I ignored them, and the fucked up thing that I continuously kicked my ass over was that I was framed for a murder that I was about to commit!

It didn't take too long for me to accept the fact that I was gonna do my stretch alone this time, until the day I heard my name during mail call. It was the happiest day that I've had in quite some time, and I even hauled ass to my cell to read my anonymous letter. I opened it and it read:

Dear, Bobby.

I've hated you so long that it feels like I've known you forever. I hope you're more comfortable than you were on the street, even though I prefer for you to be dead. But as long as you're suffering, I'm satisfied.

See, I always knew that you would dig your own grave, and that's just what you did. Oh, and don't worry about Stacy, she downspiraled after your first year in, and took to that glass dick real hard, and I did her the favor of notifying child protective services and they were just as happy to welcome that bastard child of yours to a cozy state bunk.

You never know, Bobby, one day he'll probably be your cell mate. I'll keep my fingers crossed, okay? Well, I'm not going to spend too much of my free time on your ass. A couple convict buddies of mine owe me big favors in there, and they told me that they'll look after you for me. So do me a solid and be friendly. Good luck, bitch; and think twice about leaving that prison alive, mothafucka.

Lonnie Biggs aka LB

I crumbled the letter and threw it, watching it bounce to the cell doors. I couldn't let him get in my head. All I had to do is appeal and my lawyer said I had a chance to beat the case. Besides, this was like my second home and I'm sure a lot hasn't changed since I've been here. I got off my bunk to pick up the paper when an older black male with a horrible scar on his face kicked it to the side, and leaned on my bars while he stared at me from head to toe. I didn't know him from the street and knew this wasn't a friendly visit, so I backed up before another man walked up beside "Scarface."

"We have a problem, pretty boy?"

"This ain't my first time, man, and I don't need anyone to look out for me but thanks anyway." I said and didn't get a reply afterwards.

He pulled his hands from his pockets, signaling his associate to move as well. He looked at me painfully while slowly grabbing his square from his right ear and throwing it on my bed before they began to approach me. Before I threw my hands up to prepare to rumble, while praying to God for strength to help me through my troubles, the burly man asked me if I wanted some candy.

MY KINDA GIRL . . .

Here's a Sneak Preview of:
Taking Losses

CHAPTER ONE

Sickside, Chicago

The choir silenced and the pastor spoke his peace. It hit home so hard that it made me think about the transition I've made from gangster to gentleman.

"I have something that is weighing heavy on my head today. If you don't mind, I want to get it off my chest. You see, I was putting gas in my car and there was a house next door to the gas station. On the side of the house I could see two children in the yard playing. They were pointing sticks at each other, pretending to shoot their weapons. The one child pointed the stick at the other and yelled, 'Say hello to my little friend!'

"At that moment my heart was saddened. How could it be that we have come so far just to go nowhere? How did we get to the point where we are raising our children to be gangsters, pimps, whores and drug dealers?
It was at that moment that I realized it is time for a change.

"Now I know some of you are sitting out there thinking: 'Reverend, that's easier said than done.' Well I'm here to not only tell you that you are wrong, I am going to prove it. Let's talk about the word change. Most people claim that they are trying to

change. My question is: how do you try to change? In fact, how do you try to do anything? Do you try to go to work everyday? Did you try to take a shower this morning? Are you trying to keep breathing while you are sitting here listening to me? So when you say that you are trying to change, please forgive me if it sounds a little silly to me.

"You see, change happens in an instance. Change starts when you no longer accept the way that things were. You see, most of you have the right principles, but you're in the wrong arena. Most of you are so busy following that sign that says 'shortcut this way' you fail to realize that you are going in circles. Usually by the time you get it figured out, it's too late. I'm telling you it's time for a change. That's why I want to challenge each and every one of you to vow to make a change right here and now. I want you to vow to make this village that you live in a better one. I want you to vow to be better parents so your kids can grow and make better decisions."

In the middle of the sermon I experienced a flashback that caused me to relive the years that I regret most. And this is me: Nicky Green. And this is my story.

At the age of seventeen, I was obsessed with mafia flicks and crime stories; pretending to be James Cagney, Al Pacino, Bumpy Johnson, and various other gangsters that intrigued me. Organized crime in itself, and the idea of following a code that enabled a family to stay in power, ultimately became my primary outlet to establish myself as a leader. It distinguished the difference between what I viewed as priority and what I perceived as bullshit.

I grew up on the south side streets of Chicago; the third child born to a mother of two failed marriages. A beautiful woman, indeed, who over the years, had developed a low self-esteem, yet was overwhelmed with volumes of high expectations for her kids. My teenage years were full of disappointments, but I realized the importance of principles. And that later manifested into integrity, which eventually created the man who unravels this cold story.

As a teenager I wanted it all; and like most young ghetto boys, I chose to learn my lessons the hard way. Growing up in my hood had its ups and downs, and I don't mean that with intentions to inspire the pride of affliction. But for the simple fact that my community beat me down so low that all I had left in life was to look up.

It wasn't too long before I organized a crew of my own, which consisted of Devin, Biogio, and me. These were my dogs and I would have taken two to the ribs for any of these guys! We became very close because of our similar backgrounds. And even though we earned more respect due to the less we had, we shared an unbreakable bond, that I thought couldn't be broken. But with age comes change—some for the good. But I regret to say that our intentions were all bad.

Devin was relocated to Chicago from St. Louis after witnessing his family's heartless murder. His father was a small-time drug dealer and neighborhood mechanic, who always complained about who deserved what and was filled with assumptions of what he thought he deserved. It didn't take too long before packages started to come up short, and those in question, suspiciously began to spend more money than usual. It was clear that an example had to be made, and at the expense of a supportive family, the poor decision made by the man of the house caused them to suffer the consequences of theft. Everybody had to be dealt with if a violation was rendered and the rules were broken. Unfortunately, the decision to dispose of this bloodline of thieves was approved, and through the eyes of a young and innovative little boy, even the slightest bit of mercy could jeopardize the freedom of these terrible men.

After practice, Devin had great news to tell his parents, and that day he realized why his dad was so hard on him and finally understood the result of commitment. Devin rushed home; jogging twelve blocks with one thing on his mind: the appreciation of love that his father provided which helped him overcome his doubt for the sport that he so passionately cared for. His mother would be proud to hear that her son made the starting lineup as point guard for the Madison

High Cougars. Nothing else mattered as he entered his house cautiously in preparation to surprise his parents with this great news.

After placing his book bag on the floor, Devin headed to the kitchen for a glass of juice. Upon pouring the leftover Tropicana fruit punch, he heard a suspicious and alarming sound, then a thumping beat, but didn't pay it any mind because he knew how rough his little brother played around the house.

Devin headed down the hall, eager to brag about his new position on the team that he worked so hard to accomplish. He tried to imagine the looks on their faces and the biggest smile surfaced instantly, until his moment was interrupted by his mother's scream, followed by five muffled shots. Devin dropped his glass as his body became numb from panic. The sound of the glass smashing against the hardwood floor caused the perpetrators to investigate, making it harder for him to think logically at that point.

It was only seconds before the last surviving member of the Montgomery's was face-to-face with his family's killers. One of the two men raised his hand revealing his snub-nosed, steel Ruger revolver. Before the gunman could get a shot off, the other guy grabbed his arm. "Don't! I didn't come here for this, man. It's bad enough we had to take care of the other one."

The other guy paid his words no mind and proceeded to carryout his orders.

"Take the kid in the other room and stick him quickly so we can get out of here, asshole!" He said before shoving the knife toward his partner.

Devin's feet felt like concrete and the situation sent chills down his spine, giving him courage to attempt to make it away alive. His heart pumped determination through his veins as he began to hurdle to his safety, accidentally entering the bathroom, wasting even more time than he had already.

"Hurry up, fool! He's getting away," the killer said, urging his associate to finish the job. He was just inches from Devin and had his eyes locked like a predator focused on his prey, gainfully reaching Devin close enough to grab on to his jacket. Devin squirmed out of it before entering his bedroom and through his window to escape this nightmare.

On his way to the window he ran past the lifeless body of his 6-year-old brother, lying defenseless on his twin mattress. His eyes stared upward in a trustful position and the thought of his pain contributed to an array of emotions. Seconds from safety, Devin had no time pay his proper respects.

"Help!" Devin screamed when he felt the cold air hit his face from outside. He forced himself out. Although the dangers of this stunt could've been fatal, an arm reached for him, but the killer fell short of catching Devin as the all-star basketball player leaped to save his own life. He dropped two floors down, breaking his fall on a chain-link fence, fracturing three ribs and dislocating his left shoulder. When Devin hit the ground it winded him, prohibiting his attempts to verbalize his outcry.

The impression he left to the onlookers who frequented his slum, was the vicious melody of a near-death experience. Devin's bloody appearance stained the pavement and the sound of his tragic encounter polluted the neighborhood that day. As the concerned citizens of the Robertson projects followed Devin's bloody finger, pointing directly to his newly broken home, many ran to his aid in attempt help in any way.

"Oh my God, what happened young man; who did this?" a lady asked as she held his beaten body. Devin looked at her and his eyes told the vicious tale that his mouth had no words to answer. As he lay in her arms, barely hanging on consciously, Devin couldn't stop thinking about his family, and swore that his second chance at life had to count for something.

The killers eluded capture; and out of fear for his own death, Devin was relocated by his aunt, only to establish himself in a neighborhood much worse, known as Sickside, Chicago.

For any questions or comments
Please email Michael McGrew at
legacypublishing11@gmail.com

Also:
Subscribe to my site @ www.BookBizCoach.com

About the Author

It's been a long time awaiting this moment to shine. Michael McGrew is as patient as patient can be, and has proved it over the years as a single father and businessman. After completing two seasons as a lighting technician for B.E.T in '99, he took full responsibility as a single parent to his loving son, providing and supplying the fundamental essentials that he, unfortunately, didn't have the opportunity to acquire himself as a child. It was just a year-and-a-half ago when he completed his first novel, and since then, he has completed his second, along with three children's books, story editing for two reality shows, and a screenplay. Born and raised in the south side of Los Angeles, CA, Michael McGrew's past is a living testimony that represents the epitome of struggle, and relates to many success stories heard daily.

Michael McGrew can be described in one word: Visionary. Naturally born with a gift in storytelling, writing a gripping novel is a walk in the park for this Los Angeles native. When asked about his role models and inspiration growing up, he simply explained that, "Life itself and what it offers every day is a lesson; and every lesson if learned, is the best advice the universe can give you." He is a very diverse individual with a mind that invites the reality in which we choose to either accept or ignore. We just choose to ignore the imperfections in our own perfect world.